Tales of Zo

Editors:

Andrew Byers and Chad Underkoffler

Authors:

Chad Underkoffler, Andrew Byers,
Michaelbrent Collings, Michael Hill,
Scott Kane, and Jon F. Zeigler

Tales of Zo, edited by Andrew Byers and Chad Underkoffler
Trade paperback ISBN: 978-1-62898-002-8
eBook ISBN: 978-1-62898-003-5

Cover design: http://coveryourdreams.wordpress.com/

Uncanny Books
810 West Knox St.
Durham, NC 27701
http://uncannybooks.com/

CONTENTS

The Bespectacled Boy's Introduction to the Zantabulous Land of Zo   1
Chad Underkoffler
The Blue Tailor   19
Chad Underkoffler
The Wolf Trap Picnic   30
Scott Kane
The Gingerbread Knight   45
Chad Underkoffler
Little Jack and the Yellow Dress   56
Michael Hill
The Wooden Pirate   74
Chad Underkoffler
Galen and the Golden-Coat Hare   90
Jon F. Zeigler
The Horse Prince   112
Chad Underkoffler
The Taler's Truth   121
Michaelbrent Collings
The Witch Girl   136
Chad Underkoffler
The Ship-Breaker   144
Andrew Byers
Pussycat vs. Owl   160
Chad Underkoffler
The Bespectacled ~~Boy~~ Man Returns to Zo   183
Chad Underkoffler

The Bespectacled Boy's Introduction to the Zantabulous Land of Zo

by Chad Underkoffler

My name is Jonathan Alexander King. But long ago, in another time, in another world, they called me the Bespectacled Boy.

Let me back up, not to the very beginning.

Having been evicted from my tiny Pittsburgh apartment just in time for Christmas, I found myself homeless, with only my suitcase full of clothes, my Coke-bottle glasses, and my footlocker full of books and journals. Luckily, my grandma invited me to stay with her over the holiday season, and to house-sit her cat while she went on one of her regular post-Christmas junkets to Las Vegas. After slaving over a feast worthy of Vikings for Christmas Eve, and the celebrations of Christmas Day, she and a half-dozen of her closest blue-haired old-lady friends liked to fly into Vegas on the 26th as a reward for their labors, catch some shows, play the slots, and have a jolly old time at least once a year.

"It would be a load off my mind, Jonny," she said, her grey eyes twinkling, "if you could stay here and watch Cleo while I'm gone. The poor dear gets so lonely for company." But behind the twinkle was sadness for me and my situation. She wanted to help – grandmas are like that.

Cleo – Queen Cleopatra, my grandmother's aged Siamese – liked me well enough, and I her, and (being at loose ends myself) I agreed quickly.

"Good!" she said with a grin. "You can also help me put up the Christmas decorations and tree."

I groaned to myself. Grandma Savoia always had an angle. But, dutiful – and needy! – grandson that I was, I had little problem with the work. After all, it could be fun.

I must admit that "fun" is not the right word to describe the details of decorating a large, late Victorian house owned by a grandmother who is Christmas-crazy. Boxes and boxes of tchochkes and gimcracks, ornaments and decorations, gewgaws and thingamabobs, aged electrical devices and mechanical gadgets, *all* needed to be unpacked, dusted, and set up in their historic places. I have no idea how the old girl did this every year. It took *days*, and that was with both of us going into the voluminous attic for several loads of boxes.

A few days before Christmas, while I wrestled with a tangle of ancient Christmas tree lights, she came downstairs with a strange box. "Jonny," she said, "I think this one is *yours*. It was behind Grandpa Pazzesco's old Philco radio." She presented it to me: a one foot by two foot cardboard box, mummified in masking tape. In black magic marker (you remember, the ones that smelled of licorice?), my shaky childish scrawl read: "TIME CAPSULE! Do NOT open until 2021!"

In my youth, I had been given to creating little "time capsules" that I hid hither and yon for the future. This, apparently, was one of them. (I surmise that there is at least one shoebox of Matchbox cars buried somewhere in suburban Pittsburgh, if they haven't rusted away yet.)

"Gram," I said, still busy with the tangle of lights, "just put it in my room, and I'll look at it later. Okay?"

She smiled, and did as I asked.

Unfortunately, I didn't get to look at the time capsule until after Christmas. There was too much to do: decorations to place, food to cook, family to see. (And, when you're half-Italian, that's a whole lotta family.) I didn't get a chance to properly regard the box until after I had dropped off Grandma and her cadre of gamblers at the airport for their Vegas trip.

But here I was, in a rambling old house, faced with a relic of my youth. Of course I used my pen-knife to slit the time capsule, years early. I was curious. Wouldn't you be?

Inside the box was a small stack of spiral-bound notebooks – the ones I now recalled having bought at Krause's Corner Five-and-Dime. I used to scribble in them for hours, recounting... *something*. Something I couldn't *quite* recall. This was one of my manias, preserved from those summers I spent with Grandpa and Grandma.

But.

The notebook on the top of the stack had one short word scrawled upon it, in my childhood block capitals: "**Zo**." I picked up the notebook and began to read. . . and was transported back.

The Zantabulous Land of Zo is made up of five parts.

3

There is *Azul* in the East, and *Giallo* in the West, and *Rosso* in the South, and *Viola* in the North, and *Zo Proper* in the middle. It is an empire.

My long-neglected past flooded back into me.

The Zantabulous Land of Zo! How could I have forgotten about you?

I continued to read the deliberate words of my younger self.

In Zo, there are witches, wizards, dragons, ogres, Talking Animals, Dumb Beasts, fairies, Princesses, evil step-mothers, knights. . . everything is fairytale.

I began to remember. . .

In the bedroom in Grandma Savoia's house where I traditionally slept (and where I was staying even now!), there was an **elf-door**. You know, a small, strange door, leading to somewhere unexpected. Most grown-ups would call it "access to a crawlspace," but I as a child did not accept this. It was obviously a doorway to someplace *wonderful*.

Understand: I was a dreamy lad, well-versed in Anderson and Carroll, Baum and Lang, Grimm and Disney, Lewis and Tolkien. I *desired* the wardrobe door, the whirling cyclone, the rabbit-hole to lead me to another world. The elf-door in Gram Savoia's spare bedroom seemed my best chance to enter a fairyland. So strange, tiny, and odd, it **must** lead to somewhere equally strange and odd (or so my young mind decided).

And I **had** gone to that wonderful place, been dubbed "the

Bespectacled Boy," and I had had adventures. Glorious adventures! I had returned, and written of my adventures in halting words and rough letters. This was – and is! – true.

I had also forgotten almost all about it.

This, what I am writing now, is my attempt to regain my knowledge of Zo, which I lost through fear and neglect.

Never neglect your dreams. They will uphold you in the dark.

Never dread your nightmares. They will teach you to win free of darkness.

These are lessons I failed to learn/remember as a child. I hope to relearn it as a grown-up.

In the dark, when the Savoia house was utterly quiet (between the hacksaw snores of my grandfather), a faint green light would flicker under the elf-door in my bedroom. For many nights, I was too scared to leave my warm bed. But then, one night, I got up and creeped to the door. I listened, ear against wood, and heard music. Bells and harps and trumpets and other instruments I did not know.

With a deep breath, I tried the knob. It was usually locked, but when the green light flickered, it turned easily. That singular night, I threw the door open… wide.

And stepped through, whirled in an instant into the Zantabulous Land of Zo.

Here I am now, a "grown-up" and oh-so-serious. For many years, I had chalked up my butterfly memories of Zo as fantasy, dreams. It took only a moment, after seeing my notebooks, to change my mind. Zo was *real*. I had *been* there.

I *believed* again.

As a child, I had stepped into magic one night… and my life was irrevocably changed.

Will the green light flicker at me again, this night?

Perhaps. I hope so.

The Kingdom of Azul is where I shall start transcribing my youthful notebooks. I will defer to my childlike accounts (with only a mild editing hand to better present the originals), in giving you a snapshot of Zo, as I progress through the boxful of notebooks.

Azul

The kingdom of Azul is all farmland and forest. The finest logs in Zo come from Fogwood. Many ships come to Azulite ports to get lumber, corn, potatoes, turnips, parsnips, blueleaf (I think this is like tobacco), heatwheat (it grows near the Bottomless Chasm, Azulites use it to make something like Granpa's coffee), and lotsa fruits and berries.

Azulites are hard-workers and never get tired, never quit. They wear a lot of blue, which is the official color of the kingdom.

The kingdom of Azul has no king. It is divided in two Counties: Colbaltia and Indigon. The heir to Indigon disappeared as a baby. I heard a story where they say that she was thrown into the Bottomless Chasm and is still falling to this day!

However, the witches believe that the Heir is alive, so the Counties cannot be put back together. Until the Heir is found, the villages of Indigon are run by Mayors.

Count Alphonse runs Cobaltia. He can't be King of Azul, though he really wants to be. He's very smart, but sneaky. He might be a bad guy. I've only met him once. He's really slippery, like a fish.

Famous Azulites I have met:

- The Blue Hood: She's older than me – might be a teenager? Leader of the Happy Bandits. She's a really good archer, and is always fighting with Count Alphonse.

- The Wickerwalker: It's a big scarecrow-thing made out of weeds and reeds. It stumbles around, usually smashing things in its way. But I don't think it's bad, just dumb.

- The Stitchwitch: A mean old lady who does magic with needle and thread. She tried to cut my shadow away from me! What's up with that?!?!

And, below this, in a different color of ink and a steadier hand, a later note:

The Count is trying to hire the Stitchwitch to work for him!!! He's plotting something.

Azul. Everything in Azul has a tint of the blue of a summer sky. I remember Fogwood, misty and dense. Running through the undergrowth with the Blue Hood and her men. Feasting on venison over an open campfire. Bedeviling the Count with hold-ups and silly pranks.

Slowly, I recall an adventure, where the Bespectacled Boy aided the Blue Hood in stealing Count Alphonse's underwear. *All* of his underwear. Like, weeks and weeks worth. We made a big bonfire and burned every last set, and chortled like hyenas while we did it.

She was hard, not conventionally pretty, but there was such a sense of energy and life around her. The Blue Hood brought out the best in everyone around her.

Am I too old to return to Zo?

Not dark yet. It needs to be dark for the green light to play under the elf-door. I continue to read.

An avid natural scholar, see here my youthful notes on the Talking Animals of Zo:

Talking Animals

Most of the Talking Animals in Zo stand on two legs, wear clothes, and use tools. Some don't.

If two Talking Animals of different types get married and have kids (like an Owl and a Pussycat), the boy-babies are the same as their father (Owlets) and the girl-babies are the same as their mother (Kittens).

I don't understand why some animals talk and other don't.

The Talking Animals treat the Dumb Beasts just as we do here.

It is mid-afternoon. I am reading through and transcribing my notebooks faster that I had anticipated. Again, onward.

Giallo

Giallo is where all of the grain comes from for the Zo Empire. They have a lot of Dumb Beasts, like cows. So all of the milk, cheese, bread, and leather comes from Giallo. Far to the west, over the Pancake Plains, there are other mysterious countries that sometimes send trade caravans and receive Giallon ones.

Giallons are known for their courage and common sense. Most other people of Zo think they're rude, dull, and boring. I agree. They wear a lot of yellow, which is the official color of the kingdom.

The royal family of Giallo died out a hundred years ago. Like Azul, Giallo doesn't have a single ruler. Not like Azul, instead of two counties, there are like a hundred fiefs here.

So, there are a bunch of Princes, Princesses, Dukes, Duchesses, Earls, Marchionesses, Counts, Countesses, Marquises, Marquessas, Lords, and Ladies. All of them rule part of the kingdom. They meet every two years to deal with problems.

They don't do so well with that.

The Rushing River divides Giallo from the kingdom of Viola. There are only two ways to cross the gap: the Viola Bridge and Brooz Ford.

Famous Giallons I have met:

- The Marquis de Carabas: He's a Talking Cat. Very

cultured and civilized. Maybe *too* civilized. He's a tricksy sort.

- The Roly-Poly Prince: He's a fat jerk who rules his lands like a tyrant. I don't like him.

- The Snow Witch: She stands apart from the talks of the other Giallon nobles. The one time I met her, she probably didn't even say four words. Still, she is very pretty. And very powerful. And, I think, very sad.

Giallo. Mustard-yellow fields of grain, rippling in the wind. As far as the eye can see. Farther.

I must admit that the geography of Giallo mostly bored me (all flat plains and wheat), and then suddenly surprised and delighted me with buttes, canyons, mountains, and plateaus. Pappy and Grammy King had taken me and a couple of my cousins "out West" to see the sights. I will always remember the American Midwest as a combo of **boring** interspersed with **HOLY CRAP THAT'S AWESOME**.

Giallo was **_exactly_** than that, only moreso.

Despite many times traversing Giallo's plains, I only had one adventure there. The Bespectacled Boy rescued some of the Snow Witch's retainers from the dungeons of the Roly-Poly Prince. It was easy. He was slow and stupid, and his men weren't any better. Big whoop.

However, the Snow Witch was *fascinating* to me. Beautiful, intelligent, cold, apart. I know now why I was – if I can say – attracted to her as a lad. Her shadow has stretched across my romantic life in this world.

Still not dark yet. I fear that the green light will not flicker, since I am oh so old.

Rosso! My notebooks speak of the kingdom of passion. How little I knew, because I was but a child at the time. How little I understood, but understand now.

Rosso

The kingdom of Rosso is the trading capital of the Empire. Ships set sail every day from its ports: sailing to the mysterious lands of Oversea, fishermen out to make a huge catch; and lots of pirates waylaying the traders and fishermen. On land, the farmers of Rosso grow beans, olives, lemons, oranges, limes. They also cultivate spices (like the amazingly hot *firebean*), as well as plants for dying cloth. Rossons usually wear clothes that are colored red. They are very excitable.

Famous Rossons I have met:

- <u>King Glamorgan</u>: He's Prince Charming who's lost his princess. (His wife died very young.)
- <u>Hella</u>: The Fire Fairy. Mean and nasty. Likes to make things burn.
- <u>Princess Morphea</u>: Princess, niece of Glamorgan, cursed to sleep until awakened by True Love's kiss. (20 years so far.)
- <u>Captain Mouse</u>: A pirate captain, rude in manners, but a good enough sort. (His ship is the *Rat Trap*.)

The adventurous and romantic nature of the Rossons confused me as a child. You must understand: passion rules Rosson thoughts and deeds – they feel everything *intensely* (and often loudly).

Nowhere is this more evident than during the annual *Crimson Festival*. It runs for three consecutive nights, lasting from midnight to dawn. Revelers go masked and costumed to hundreds of galas and fetes. A sense of misrule pervades the celebrations – anything can (and does!) happen during Festival. Carousing, dueling, and seducing attractive members of the preferred sex are par for the course.

Rosso is where emotions run riot. Be warned. Less tempting for a child, more tempting for a teen or an adult.

Let us move on, onto the kingdom of magic… Viola.

Viola

Viola is a country, full of mountains. Lots of hill villages in lush valleys. Most of the mining of the Zo Empire happens here. Copper, tin, iron, gold, silver, and other metals are found in its mountains. It also produces marble. Violan apples are nearly as good as Azulite ones, but the Violander purplepear is more flavorful than any other – juicy, delicious, almost like a nectarine. Violander goats – Dumb Beasts not Talking Animals – produce milk that makes a yummy cheese. The Rushing River flows out of Windy Gap and divides Viola from its neighbor Giallo.

Violanders wear a lot of purple.

Famous Violanders I have met:

- Princess Paige: Likes books more than I do! Alas, she studies more than she rules.
- Quellabaum: King of the Flying Monkeys who live

on Razor Peak; kinda a snob, but a good guy – he carried me four leagues through the air to stop the Army of Clay before they attacked the Wool People.

- Stig: A barbaric ogre overlord who wants to be king of Viola. Jerk.

The Violanders I met in my youthful peregrinations were all smart and inventive. Viola is one of the most accepting places in the Empire to live (perhaps even more than the cosmopolitan Jade City in Zo Proper).

I had never seen a land as well-tended as Zo Proper, and I had never seen a city as large as the Jade City. I was quite overwhelmed. There were people and things there I had never imagined. (Take a kid from East Boonies, PA, and drop him into NYC – that's the kind of reaction I had.)

Zo Proper

Zo Proper is the metropole of the Zo Empire, and the personal holding of the Zorcerer of Zo Him-/Her-/Itself. He/She/It rules from Jade City. The fields of Zo Proper are covered in brilliant green flowers called bottleblooms, and a more useful plant cannot be found. Bottlebloom flowers can be drained of copious amounts of sweet, effervescent nectar, and then the blossoms can be dried and eaten as candy. The seeds of the plant are nutritious and filling. The stalks can be used directly in weaving, or processed in one way to produce paper and in another to produce cloth. The leaves are a tasty preservative herb, and can also be dried and burned like incense. The hills of Zo Proper support greenfleece sheep, Dumb Beasts with exceedingly fine, smooth, silky wool. Strange opaque gems called fenjades are often found in its swampier regions. The livery of Zo Proper is green; Imperial livery is green and gold.

Zolanders are known for their keenness of observation and exquisite manners. They also excel at writing, singing, acting, painting, sculpture, and other artistic pursuits. Indeed, anything requiring attention to detail is fair game for a Zolander; they make the finest jewelry, the best clocks, and the most ingenious toys. Fashions are made and broken in Jade City, and nearly every wealthy or powerful individual in the entire Empire has or desires to have a small house there. Many of the movers and shakers of the Empire have attended Lime University, located within the Jade City. However, their overwhelming politeness and mannered speech leads many other inhabitants of other Kingdoms to see them as insincere, pretentious, or inscrutable.

Famous Zolanders I have met:

- <u>The Smiling Soldier</u>: Captain of the Imperial Guard and valiant knight.

- <u>Ilsa Hund</u>. Famed minstrel and gossip-monger.

- <u>The Zorcerer of Zo</u>: He/She/It is a mystery. Despite centuries of rule, few have seen the sovereign of the land. No one knows if this being is male or female, or human or Talking Animal. Audiences with the Zorcerer are rare.

   While He/She/It rules from Jade City in theory, in practice the Zorcerer rarely exercises power directly. Instead, the Zorcerer works through trusted agents, like the Smiling Soldier and other Imperial officers and Ministers. When the Zorcerer does issue direct commands to His (Her? Its?)

subjects, they are usually transmitted by Imperial letter, writ on creamy green paper, in dark green ink, impressively sealed and beribboned, and carried by a Dumb Beast courier that glows faint green.

The Zorcerer uses the royal "we" when referring to Himself (Herself? Itself?).

On those few occasions when the Zorcerer is thought to take a direct hand, there is thunder, lightning, fire, winds, great confusion, and a dramatic, huge effect. (It's rumored that there once was a village that refused to follow the Zorcerer's edicts. . . It's better known now as the Bottomless Chasm.)

Who is the Zorcerer?

No one knows. Here are some theories:

- *Clockwork Man.* Some Zolanders believe the Zorcerer is an antique Clockwork Man, who has learned strange new mechanical magics.

- *Jack.* Many people claim that the Zorcerer is really the famous Jack, hero of the Empire. His stories are legend. That Jack: Jack Be Nimble, Jack & the Beanstalk, the Jack who went up the Hill with Jill, Jack the Giant-Killer, Jack Spratt who could eat no fat.

- *No one.* A few iconoclasts hold that there is no Zorcerer at all, but is a front used by others – like the Smiling Soldier – to keep the peace between the powerful nobles of the Kingdoms.

- *Otherworlder.* Some wizards and witches hold that the Zorcerer is an Otherworlder come to Zo, using strange Otherworldly magics to work his (her? its?) will and rule the Empire.

- *Shaykosch*. A handful of lunatics believes that Shaykosch, the Deathless Wolf, is really the Zorcerer. He rules with an iron fist to provide himself with a private playground of horror and destruction.

- *Somebody Innocuous*. The Zorcerer is just some person (probably a commoner, possibly a Talking Beast, Living Toy, or Living Confection) that couldn't rule outright because of the nature of their birth, their appearance, or the nature of their existence.

- *Zolion*. Some Zolanders think the Zorcerer is the first savior of Zo, Zolion, now immortal but very aged. Some folks think the Zorcerer is the ghost of Zolion, hanging around to make sure all is well!

The Return of the Wolf

In a fairytale land, how scary must a bedtime story be to frighten even the doughtiest hero? Invariably, such a story revolves around the Gray Wind, Murder on Four Legs, the Immortal One: **Shaykosch**, the Deathless Wolf.

It is said that Shaykosch has once again returned from the grave. He and his numerous wicked followers sow discord throughout the Zantabulous Land of Zo. Beast, sorcerer, and shapeshifter, he stalks the land and wreaks havoc, trying to sate his all-consuming hunger.

While a new hero puts the Wolf down every few decades, eventually the monster rises again in the huffing and puffing wind.

The Blue Tailor stopped him once, stitching his shadow to a rock with magic needle and thread, then dropping the rock into Bottomless Chasm. The Wooden Pirate filleted him on the Southern Sea, scattering the Wolf's guts as chum for the Lightning Sharks. Another time, the Horse Prince trampled him into the muddy fields of Giallo after a long, running battle. Theodora the Witch Girl matched him spell for spell, and finally triumphed. And there are a dozen other tales and deaths and returns.

Who will stop him the next time? And how? Will some brave soul beg the Zorcerer to stretch forth his power? Or would collecting the magical weapons used against Shaykosch in the past be helpful? Who knows?

And that was the end of my childhood notebooks.

It was finally dark.

I decided to go upstairs, to my traditional bedroom.

I am sitting on the bed, right now, looking at the elf-door, writing in this notebook, waiting for the green glow to shine around its edges. I am simultaneously scared and thrilled.

. . .

Fear and anticipation are overrated.

. . .

The Moon has just risen above the horizon; I can see it from the single window in my traditional room. It's silvery and nice.

. . .

A noise! The lock on the elf-door just unlocked itself!

And now the green glow.

The door is swinging open. The Bespectacled ~~Boy~~ Man is apparently needed in Zo.

(Gram, I left two days food and water for Cleo, you should be back tomorrow, so no worries.)

Much love,

Jonny

The Blue Tailor

by Chad Underkoffler

Once Upon A Time, in the Land of Zo. . .

In the kingdom of Azul, there lived a tailor and his wife. They were poor but happy and expecting their first child. This made them feel richer – and happier – than any gold or silver could. Indeed, it may be true that they were even happier than King Cerulan, who was to wed the Princess Charma at the end of the month.

For weeks before the royal wedding, the tailor worked fixing, fitting, and fancifying the garments new and old of his neighbors, both noble and common. All wished to look their best for the gala ball after the King's nuptials.

The tailor was thankful for the work, since his wife was great with child, and any extra earnings he made during this time would support his growing family in leaner times. The rich paid him in silver, the merchants paid him in trade, and the poor paid him in chickens and loaves and butter and ale.

Through all of this the tailor found the time, the cloth, the thread, and the beads to make his wife a flattering and beautiful dress for the festival. (In Azul, all subjects were invited to share in the royal joy by tradition.)

Alas – that dress was not to be worn to the ball by the tailor's wife, for she went into labor as the last rays of sunset faded from the skies and the chapel bell began to peal, calling the Azulites of the town to the wedding ceremony.

The tailor was in a state. The midwife had already left her cottage for the chapel – *everyone* had left their homes for the chapel – and he didn't want to risk running over and leaving his wife alone with the baby imminent. He tried to boil some sheets and tear up clean water, but that wasn't working so well. So he went to hold her hand, soothe her brow, and feel helpless. The child was coming. Now.

Just then, there was a knock at the door. He sprang up and found a haggard old witch dressed in torn rags standing on his front step.

"Mend my shift, so I may go to the royal wedding," she said to the tailor.

"My wife is in childbed now, good mother, and I cannot leave her to pick up needle and thread. I am truly sorry," replied the tailor.

"I can sit with here and aid her as you set to your work," said the crone. "I've overseen the birth of many a bairn with these old eyes, and held many a squalling sweetie in these gnarled arms."

Thankful for her offer, the tailor showed the witch into the bedroom, where his wife lay panting. The old woman placed her wrinkled hand on the wife's brow, mumbled some magic words under her breath, and the wife's pain obviously and immediately became more bearable. She smiled up at the witch and her husband before dozing off.

"To your work," commanded the witch, shedding her rags, stripping down to a pure white chemise that draped her gnarled but sturdy body. The tailor took the bundle of oddments and stepped into his workroom.

Laying out the old woman's rags, he quickly saw that there was little that he could do with them. They were old, threadbare, torn, dirty, patched-upon-patches. He sighed on the witch's behalf – this was the best she had to wear to the ball, and there was no time to make them presentable.

Before he could despair, his eye lighted upon the dress he had made for his wife, hanging in the corner of the room. Without hesitation, he took down the dress and placed it on his worktable. For surely, he said to himself, he and his wife and his newborn child would not attend the ball this evening, so at least the dress he had made would. Taking measurements from the witch's ratty gown, he altered his wife's present to fit the old woman's frame.

As he tied off and snipped the last bit of thread from the reworked dress, he heard a baby's cry. The dress still in hand, he rushed into the bedroom to see mother and child – a son! he had a son! – crying in relief. The witch stood next to the bed, beaming down at the pair.

The tailor pushed the dress into the crone's hand without even a glance at her, then bent down over his wife to kiss her forehead. After that his eyes were only for his son. He sat down on the bed, lost in love for his family for a timeless time.

A soft harrumph brought him back to the moment. He turned to see the witch, now wearing the altered dress. Instead of a hunched old crone, there stood a tall, straight woman, handsome as they say, of advanced years. She looked lovely.

The witch, with tears in her eyes, said, "This is too much. I cannot pay."

"Old mother, consider it thanks for your help with the delivery. Accept it as a gift of our joy."

"It is still too much."

"It is not enough."

The witch sighed, but she also smiled. "I thank you, tailor, for this generous gift. I cannot repay you in gold or silver, but I can give you and your family my blessing." She spoke magic words of benison over the little family, then kissed the infant upon the brow and whispered something that sparkled and crackled into his tiny pink ear. The baby cooed and laughed.

The witch then left for the chapel, getting there just in time to see the King and the Princess kiss. At that point, the royal gala commenced, but it is said that despite the great joy that rollicked through Azul that night, none were happier than the tailor's family within their tiny cottage.

They named the boy Bernard, because he had the same steely-gray, sharp eyes as the tailor's wife's father (who, by the by, was a weaver the next village over). But that is not what everyone called the child. For you see, when his hair finally grew, it was the color of the early spring sky: a pale blue, with streaks of soft gray-white. Thus, the tailor's son became known to all as Blue.

Even before he could talk, Blue could work with needle, thread, and scissors like a boy twice his age. By the time he could talk, he was as skilled as his father. Furthermore, his eye for cloth, color, and cut rivaled that of his mother, the talented child of a family of weavers herself. By the normal time of apprenticeship, Blue was already turning out masterpieces of stitching, embroidery, and tailoring.

The tailor and his wife were overjoyed at their son's ability, and with Blue's fine work and attention to detail, their fortunes rose.

Eventually they were not poor any longer, but rather well-off.

That's when Blue, his talents ever increasing, broke a china dish when his mother was out to market and his father bent over a tricky bit of needlework on the King's torn pantaloons. As Blue swept up the shards of the plate, he had an idea. Rather than throwing the pieces away, he dumped them on his little workbench in the corner of the room. Taking his thinnest, finest steel needle, he blew softly on the point. Then, he threaded it with the finest Overseas silk passed through the steam of the whistling teakettle. Strange, new, known-but-unknown words played upon his lips, and he spoke them under his breath as he set to work.

When the tailor had finished with the King's pantaloons, he turned to see what his son was doing. His eyes widened like teacups in surprise: Blue was stitching together the shards of china! The stitches were fine, invisible, unnoticeable, nonexistent – but the plate held together, not even a crack showing where the boy's needle and thread had passed! Blue set the last piece into place, made seven quick stitches, and bit off the thread.

The plate was whole, unbroken, like new, perfect.

And that was just the beginning.

The skill of the Blue Tailor was so great that he could mend a shattered friendship, sew up a broken heart, or even place a stitch in time to save nine. He could draw together things torn asunder so well none could ever know they had been separated. He could hem and dart unequal relationships, so they fit all more perfectly. He could embroider situations to best advantage.

Yet, through all of this, Blue never became proud or boastful or abusive. He used his magic to mend and fix, to repair and beautify, to make whole and sound. He was happiest at his work: plying cloth with needle, a party with a song, or troubles with sound advice. His character was as remarkable as his powers, and his powers were great.

And those powers are what brought Shaykosch to Azul.

One evening, as Blue returned to his house from stitching up the miller's broken arm, he found the door wide open and swinging in the unseasonably chill wind.

He entered the cottage (and thus the workroom) to find a gigantic gray wolf sitting atop his quivering, terrified parents. Its weighty haunches pinned their bodies to the ground underneath, while its massive front paws covered their mouths. Their eyes pleaded with Blue to run, run away, escape, and leave them to their fate.

"You are the Blue Tailor, I trust?" asked Shaykosch, Death On Four Legs.

Though scared to the bones, Blue forced words from his mouth. "I am."

"Younger than I expected. No matter. I have a task for you that requires your nimble needle." The wolf smiled, displaying a mouthful of razor-white fangs. "Refuse, and your parents die. Then you die. Then everyone in this village dies." The wolf laughed. "I am *very* hungry."

Blue steeled himself. "And if I do as you ask?"

The wolf narrowed his eyes of green fire. "Then only *you* die. These two tasty morsels" – he indicated the squashed tailor and his wife – "and the rest of them shall be spared."

Swallowing hard, Blue nodded. "So be it. What requires my eyes, my fingers, my needle, my thread, my scissors?" As he said the last word, an idea sparked.

The wolf tossed his head and said, "Look at my shadow."

In the flickering lamplight of the workroom, Blue saw Shaykosch's shadow printed on the wall. It was torn in two, both halves dancing separately in the glow of the wick. They snarled and snapped at each other, locked in combat behind the Gray Wolf's back.

"The foul zorcery of that *fool* did this to me," growled the wolf. "The Zorcerer caught me unawares as I was eating the hamlet of Madder West in Rosso. Like a coward, he struck me from behind. I ran. My torn shadow limits my power, so I cannot make him pay until it is fixed."

The wolf leaned forward, and as he spoke Blue was struck by his abattoir breath. "Until you fix it."

Blue's fingers reached behind his back and found his silver scissors. They curled around the handle-loops of the sharp – impossibly sharp – blades (for Blue honed them himself until they could slice through butter without leaving a visible line). He began to sweat, screwing up his courage for the ultimate risk.

"Stop." Said the wolf, pushing down on his father's face, drawing a muffled groan from the tailor. "Though I am too weak to take on the Zorcerer, little Blue Tailor, I am strong and fast enough to kill everyone in this cottage before you can even lift those shiny scissors."

Blue let his scissors clatter to the table. He sighed, and said, "I will do as you wish. But I cannot fix your shadows here or now. The light is too inconsistent, the wall is too broad, and they are too agitated to stand still long enough."

"This is all true. So, what is to be done?"

"We must have a place where the light is strong and steady and clear. A place with limited space for them to move. A time when they are sluggish and slow."

"Do you know such a place, such a time?" asked Shaykosch.

Blue thought a moment, a plan knitting together in his head. "I do. The Lonely Finger, at sunrise."

The Lonely Finger was a bit of rock that jutted out over the edge of Azul's Bottomless Chasm. Only the bravest souls crept out upon it, to listen to the howling winds of the Chasm or to peer down into the darkness to try and see if there was a bottom far below.

It was a long and fearsome night. The Wolf's stomach grumbled loudly, his jaws dripped with slaver, and his fiery eyes lit upon father, mother, and son with such a hungry light that it was almost unbearable.

No one slept.

Blue's parents shivered in terror. The Grey Wind grinned in malevolence. The Blue Tailor sat, honing his scissors, selecting his needles, and preparing his thread.

Before sunrise the next day, Blue and Shaykosch stood near where the Lonely Finger met the edge of the Bottomless Chasm.

"I shall stand out on the Finger," began Blue. "When the sun rises over there, above the leaves of the Oribori Forest, nothing will obstruct its light. Your shadows will be crisp and clear, and have no room to move because of the narrow space. They will also be sluggish as they awaken from the sleep of night. I will be able to stitch them together easily."

Shaykosch nodded. "And then I will gobble you up, but leave your parents and village to mourn you." The wolf grinned evilly. "And don't think you can push me off the edge. I outweigh you sevenfold, tailor."

Blue shook his head. "I know I cannot push you off."

"And do not try to stab me with your silver scissors. As I said last night, I am seven times stronger than you."

"I know you are mightier."

"Nor can you outrun me, for I am the Gray Wind, seven times faster than the hurricane."

"I know you are swifter than I. And furthermore, you'll be blocking my path, for you need to stand in the middle of the Finger between the sun and I."

The sky began to turn rosy.

Shaykosch said to the Blue Tailor, "Dawn approaches. Get out there and get ready."

Blue knelt on one knee and fiddled with his shoe. "Just let me tie my laces."

The wolf rolled his eyes, looking over the Oribori Forest to gauge the rising of the sun.

At that moment, Blue's fingers flashed, pulling a needle from inside his sleeve, the steel sliver dipping into the rock once, twice, thrice – three quick stitches. Then, in a twinkle, the needle was back up in his cuff, before the wolf's gaze turned back to him.

"Ready now?"

"Yes." Blue stood, marched straight out onto the Finger, and turned to wait upon the sun.

Dawn was not long in coming.

Blue stood on the tip of the Finger, rock crumbling away to fall into the abyss at his feet. The outcrop swayed slightly in the howling winds.

As the sun rose above Oribori, he squatted with needle at the ready. It was threaded with spider silk twisted with fog, treated in magical ways he had come to understand.

The two shadows grew from the wolf, stretching out lazily from his haunches, reaching towards the Blue Tailor. They were dulled, fuzzled, still half asleep.

Blue reached forward, his fingers flickering, his needle knitting them together in a blur. Even Shaykosch's fiery green eyes couldn't follow their movement – and thus missed that with every third stitch, the Blue Tailor's needle again dipped below ground, attaching the shadow to the rock of the Lonely Finger.

In minutes, the task was done, and the wolf's two shadows were once again one. With a flourish, Blue snipped off the thread with his silver scissor and stood. Waiting.

Shaykosch stretched and shifted, and his shadow, once again under his command, shifted along with him.

"Good work. Come here for your payment." He opened his slavering jaws to consume the Blue Tailor.

"I'd rather not," said Blue, standing his ground.

"Don't make me come out there," growled the wolf.

Blue brandished his silver scissors, but did not move his footing. "No."

"You are a fool. A brave fool, true, but a fool nonetheless. You are also breakfast."

The wolf took a step forward, further along the Finger. The Blue Tailor had nowhere to run.

"Your shiny scissors won't even scratch my throat when I swallow you." Another step.

Blue said nothing.

"You may as well fall, for you cannot escape me any other way."

"Oh, I think I can," replied Blue, and then he leapt into the air, *towards* the wolf. Blue landed with great force, a scant pace from Shaykosch, close enough to smell the graveyard dirt of the monster. There was a low cracking noise, and the Finger swayed ominously.

For a moment, the wolf was stunned, and reared back. As his heavy paws thumped on the Finger, it swayed even more, and the cracking noises became louder, more earnest, sounding off like a string of fireworks.

"You've killed us both!" howled the wolf, losing his footing as the Finger snapped off of the edge, and dropped into the Bottomless Chasm, causing them both to fall.

"No, just you," said Blue, as the invisible thread he had stitched into the top of the chasm when he tied his shoe earlier stopped his descent.

Shaykosch bellowed in rage and fear as he tumbled into the darkness, lost to the world for a span of years.

The Blue Tailor climbed up his thread like a nimble spider and cut himself free. He returned to the village to find his parents and neighbors – and himself! – safe and uneaten.

He lived a long, happy, adventurous life after vanquishing the Gray Wolf. . . but that's another tale.

THE END

The Wolf Trap Picnic

by Scott Kane

Once Upon A Time, in the Land of Zo. . .

The day the Zolander semi-Windsday Grassy Field Bubble Picnic and Goodtime Marshmallow Jamboree erupted with screaming children would haunt Hipparcos to the end of his hippopotamus days. In fact, it even surpassed that time he had accidentally stumbled into the cave full of slap bats and drop bears near the end of his Reflective Meditation Journey. And, as if the Jamboree memory wasn't already etched deeply enough in his thoughts, two of the four webbed toes on his right foot still ached from a wild hammer blow, so that every time he took a step, there was Shaykosch still ... well, stepping on his toes.

But let us back up to the start of this hammer-toed hoedown, since this *particular* Jade City Jamboree was one that would be recounted for several generations and even immortalized in song by Ilsa Hund's choral litter.

That year's Jamboree took shape due to some ill-considered boasting by the Roly-Poly Prince of Giallo. While visiting Jade

City, the Prince's wayward wooing of Imperial Minister Jellia floundered badly when he had implied her generous girth was due to wolfing down Giallo's famous Banana Canary Daffodil muffins – or was it Canana Berry? Regardless, the flaming slap of her emerald glove had quickly alerted the rotund royale to his Pancake Plains-sized *faux pas*. Before he could salvage any scrap of dignity or diplomacy, Minister Jellia had decreed to all within hearing distance that the Rainbow Ribbon – a highly sought-after annual culinary award – for that year's sweetest treat would be determined in two weeks' time at the Grassy Field Bubble Picnic in Zo Proper; and in a less loud, but somehow equally overheard voice, she had suggested that the Prince could – not to put too fine a point on it – store his muffins elsewhere.

And so the Rainbow Ribbon Panel of Judges was quickly convened with a representative from each of the four lands surrounding Zo Proper: King Quellabaum, ruler of the flying monkeys of Razor Peak in far northern Viola, the Queen Blue Hood from Azul to the east, Princess Joyeux from Rosso to the south (yes, still a princess after all these years), and somewhat controversially, the thoughtless Roly-Poly Prince himself from Giallo to the West. In the event of a tie, Imperial Minister Jellia from Zo Proper would cast the final vote herself.

Now, while Hipparcos was never one to pass up a picnic of any sort, when he heard about this event, he knew he needed to taste each of the finest sweets and confections that Zo had to offer. It was sheer luck that he was in Jade City that week on other business. A bottle of the sticky purple Violan honey (and maybe the green bottlebloom candies – those were pretty good too) would be a good complement to his traveling tea kit, and positively serene when dolloped into his personal blend of Rosson red watercress tea.

Sweets had always been Hipparcos' weakness. An intimidating presence with a stout frame and thick limbs, the crimson-robed

Talking Hippopotamus had ascended the ranks of the Order of the Mirror and had been tutored in his youth by the venerable Sir Horace Hogg himself. The white cuffs, edges, and piping on the red robe denoted him as a Rosson who had journeyed throughout all the lands of Zo, although some Lime University scholars had frustrated themselves trying to prove that the frosted trim instead denoted Mirror Mages who had survived an additional apprenticeship under Hogg's wife, the Snow Queen. The Order was notoriously paranoid about their particular practices, and they held on to their secret knowledge even tighter than the wide black belt that cinched Hipparcos' robes. An impressively large and intricately inscribed silver buckle plate was the only extravagance on his otherwise modest outfit.

Unfortunately for Hipparcos and many other Jamboree-ers that day, the picnic had exercised its inexorable right to attract unwelcomed visitors: The whiskers of Shaykosch, the Deathless Wolf, had also caught wind of the sweet feast.

Hidden among the afternoon clouds, the Wolf King surveyed the pavilions being assembled below on the Grassy Field fairgrounds and reasoned thusly:

> I am very hungry, and this large collection of exceptional and magically delicious foods could momentarily sate my ravenous belly. Should I still be hungry, there will be a large selection of plump children that cannot run very fast. And after that, if there is room, why there is even a well-stocked petting zoo of Dumb Beasts right here on the outskirts at the bottom of the hillock. Once I am full, I could even cause some havoc right in the middle of Jade City, a few minutes run to the west. This is a very good plan indeed.

Later that evening as the Moon began to rise, an oily wind slid from among the clouds and spilled into the shadows among the booths.

*　　*　　*

The next morning as the sun rose over the Grassy Field, the bubble bees were released, earnestly carbonating the early autumn Jamboree air. Small children chased after the bubbles, as the older picnickers caught up with rarely-seen friends. The bakers and chefs from far and wide were busy putting the finishing touches on their colorful Jamboree masterpieces, and the vendors were readying their booths with eye-catching tablecloths and paints. A few of the greenfleece sheep contentedly munching grass in the petting zoo sneezed loudly when the bubbles landed on their noses. No one noticed when the rather surly buckthorn green sheep near the edge of the pen gulped a mouthful of the bees and licked its lips.

Many officials had either decided to make the journey to the Jamboree, or they – like Hipparcos – had already been in Jade City for other stuffy, boring reasons. Most came for the excellent food, but a few wanted to see the Roly-Poly Prince receive some come-uppance, since they too – at one time or another over the years – had tasted his peculiar brand of in-your-face diplomacy. Queen Paige from Viola was there, as well as the ironsmith Vang Lief from Ironshoe, less than a day's bumpy cart ride to the northeast. Even from the far away Island of Forgotten Toys, off the eastern shores of Viola, Baron Deril had sent a host of nesting dolls, very likely instructed to return un-nested and packed full of treats.

It is said that Vang Lief, the gruff Talking Bear with the iron hammer, had a certain fondness for Jamborees, and if plied with enough heatwheat ale from the eastern farmlands of Azul, he would burst into a furry flurry of foot-stomping songs about honey, bandanas, and musical instruments of questionable origin. And should any biscuits drizzled with Violan violet honey appear, why then the grizzled smith would make those biscuits disappear just as quickly. But as entertaining as a dancing bear can be, this is not Vang Lief's story today – that is another tale.

Near mid-day, the culinary carnival hit its stride. Children and smaller Zolanders alike nimbly scurried under foot, hoof, paw, claw, and the occasional wooden leg to taste everything they could. The Azulberry pie booth seemed particularly popular as evidenced by the amount of blue-stained smiles in the crowd. Aknow the Candysmith's journeyman was also doing a brisk business in her tent; a good sign. The cart-mounted pipe organ, which could trace its lineage back to the first Goodtime Marshmallow Jamboree, had been wheeled out to the field and was whistling its merry tunes. Right next to it, the Marshmallow Moon Bounce was filled with children madly bouncing in all directions. It served both as a quick rest for already-exhausted parents and as a sugar-driven bellows for the pipe organ.

Long ago, the "marshmallow" portion of the Jamboree consisted of medicinal booths where hedgecrafters plied their herbalism and healing goods. The swamp-grown mallow herb proved to be a popular picnic remedy, both to those who had over-indulged on food, and to those who had forgotten to bring a floppy hat for the sunshine. To quiesce queasiness, the herb was used as a gummy drink; and to soothe sunburn, it was used as a poultice. The less scrupulous and more enterprising herbalists began selling the "marsh mallows" as a confection alongside their medicines, which caused a surely- unrelated increase in their sales for stomach remedies. Some credit the idea to the parasol witch who had occasionally popped in, but in any case, a spoonful of sugar really did help the medicine go down (and help the moneybags pile up).

As the years passed, the herbalist section had transformed more and more into a candy land. While the occasional unguent could still be bought at the timeworn "Salve the Day" booth, the green-flamed Z'mores had become the real draw. Games and attractions were added to keep the older children and parents nearby, and there was always sledding on the marshmallow snow. There was even a contest for which toasted marshmallow looked the most like the Zorcerer (actually the contest served as a means for the Zorcerer to find promising clairvoyant youths, but that, too, is another tale).

The Imperial Ministers had also added their own ridiculous games of Fluffy Bunny to the mix as a means to appeal to the commoners. The game involved successive rounds of the Ministers each placing a marshmallow into their mouth and then trying to say "fluffy bunny" until they were judged unintelligible. While the Ministers thought this was hilarious, the fair-goers usually declared that the bureaucrats were unintelligible to begin with and then walked off in search of the Z'mores.

And this year's picnic was no different. There were plenty of Z'mores toasting over the fires, the sun was shining, the floppy hats were out, and the tables and booths had been piled high with some of the best morsels Zo had to offer. People were chatting amiably as they wandered the fair in search of the next delicious wonder. Some scallywag had even loosed the Dumb Beasts from the petting zoo. A joyously jumbled and sticky time was being had by all.

All throughout the candy booths, a string of children chased after the buckthorn green sheep as it caromed off the fair-goers and tables. The sheep seemed to take particular glee in ramming unsuspecting folks from behind, bleating wetly, belching a gray smoky bubble, and then disappearing into the crowd again. The bubbles hovered at shoulder height and resisted both the gentle breeze and the children's grasping hands. Had anyone been observing from above, the sheep's indirect path about the field could have easily been followed via the rippling crowd and indignant gasps. They would also have noticed the bubbles' discreet placement near the edges of the crowd.

The Wolf's belly could take no more of the wondrous aromas and succulent children. It made him want to swallow the very sunlight. So before his growling gut could give him away, he sprung his trap. With a final dash between Queen Paige's knees and through her royal purple dress and lavender petticoats (causing her to land in a less-than-regal manner), the buckthorn green sheep bounded off a table to land atop a booth. The sheep reared up, and the Wolf unfurled his true form in a swirl of green wool and gray wind.

At the same time, the Wolf's reflection coalesced from his dark breath within each of smoky bubbles bobbing at the edges of the Jamboree. Those closest to the bubbles naturally recoiled at visage of the Deathless One appearing so abruptly in front of them. Children screamed and hid behind their mothers' skirts or under nearby tables. Those closest to the Gray Wind's improvised pie booth podium did the same. Swords were loosed from their sheaths and bakers clenched their rolling pins. Distantly, in Jade City, horns trumpeted an alarm. While the smoky bubbles spun in place, a wind began whirling just beyond them, quickly creating a blurry wall that prevented any escape. The result was a panicked ring of Zolanders ripe for the Wolf's plucking.

"Now I can truly feast on all the flavors on this land." The Wolf King menaced his captive audience simultaneously from his perch and from his reflection in the bubbles corralling the crowd. "I think my infernal hunger could be sated for a moment this day!"

At the foot of that very same booth, Vang Lief had been taking advantage of the shade to have a nice heatwheat ale (or three) until his reverie had been interrupted by all the thumping and slavering above. The Talking Bear uneasily clambered onto the barrel beside the booth and started at finding the Wolf on the roof. He yanked his hammer from his belt and swung it wildly at the intruder, but Vang Lief missed terribly. The Wolf adeptly leapt off the pie booth and away from the surprise attack. The smith's hammer slipped from his unprepared grip, smashed through the adjoining wooden stall, and mashed Hipparcos squarely on top of his right foot, causing him to bellow and hop backwards into a chilled tub of Indigon iced cream cakes.

Now on the ground again, the Gray Wind swirled and darted amongst the crowd scattering people, wooden benches, greenfleece sheep, and pastries with equal malice, causing ten times the amount of destruction that he had caused in his wooly emerald costume. Not wasting an opportunity, any airborne pastries were snatched in midflight by his vicious maw. The Sideways Cakes sprinkled with faerie dust were even less of a challenge for they tended to float in the air on their own. While it abated his hunger momentarily, the Deathless Wolf knew it would not last long, especially with his master plan tipped alee. He needed more. He sprang from stall to stall gluttonously gulping whole loaves of bread and buckets of apples at a time. Still, it was not enough.

A hot wash of cider cleared his throat for a bone-chilling howl, freezing many nearby picnickers in their tracks and allowing the Wolf an idle turn on the trampled grass. Sniffing out his next snack, a glow caught his eye.

And there it was, a giant golden mound cresting the hill like the yellow morning sun: the Banana Canary Daffodil Muffins. The devil bread that had (really through no fault of its own) started this whole mess, drizzled with thick sticky strips of Violan honey. The Wolf rapaciously descended on the muffins with horrible gobbling sounds.

Hipparcos shook his foot free of the ice tub and turned on his tree trunk legs to face the trampled remains of the Jamboree. He deliberated for a moment, pushing aside the pain from his throbbing foot, and focused his mind.

He had heard Master Hogg's tales of his own encounter with Shaykosch many times, but Hipparcos had always thought that the tale had grown in the re-telling. Seeing the gray evil firsthand chilled him to his core. But Hipparcos knew the Blue Hood in her pre-Queen days had defeated the Wolf, and he had thought he had seen her earlier that day near the dart toss booth, so he searched the crowd for her colors. There she was! – across the field surrounded by a small dense pack of her Indigo Infantry trying their best to keep their Queen at maximum distance from Shaykosch.

Hipparcos lumbered across the field, red sweat beading on his brow. The Queen Blue Hood noted the people clearing a path for Hipparcos, anticipated the Talking Hippopotamus' plan, and moved to intercept him.

Before Hipparcos could catch his breath and bow to address her, the Queen said "I know what you are going to ask of me, Mirror Mage. While it is true I helped your master dispatch that beast years ago, the Wooden Pirate has been understandably reluctant to sacrifice any more limbs to create another wolfslaying arrow. I can spare a few of my sword arms for closer combat, while I nettle him with this sad excuse for a bow." With a subtle flick of her wrist, she indicated the weakly-strung Apple Arrow carnival game bow at her side.

"No matter, your Majesty, I know you will do what you can. It seems Master Hogg did not exaggerate Shaykosch's menace."

The Queen stared at the melee surrounding the Wolf atop the hill. "He did not. Your master would not have been capable of any untruths after our last encounter with the Wolf." As her Indigo Infantry urged her away, the Queen had one last thought. "Zolion be with you, mage."

On the opposite side of the crowd, the Monkey King had had enough nonsense for one day. He cocked his rumpled black derby lower on his brow with one hand, while knuckling his stogie between his yellowed teeth. He puffed three times, causing the end of his cigar to wink like an ominous red eye. He casually leaned towards the closest smoky bubble and said, "Here's what I tink a yer mangy mutt threats." With a poke of his blueleaf cigar, King Quellabaum popped the lurid sphere right where the Wolf's nose was reflected.

Chaos erupted as the greasy bubbles burst in unison. The hurricane fence dissipated, and the festival-goers scattered in all directions. The Monkey King propelled himself backwards and upwards above the picnic pandemonium with a quick sweep of his wings, his derby crown not disturbed in the least by the sudden motion.

Hipparcos was startled by the sudden dissipation of the wind wall, but at least the picnickers could put some distance between themselves and the Wolf. Ever since being initiated into the Order of the Mirror, it had been hammered into the young recruits that they existed to combat the Deathless One. Hipparcos grimaced as he realized that thought's "they" had just been boiled down to "he" – this would his responsibility today. He steeled himself, unlatched the elaborate belt plate from its frame, and flipped it open to reveal a large hexagonal mirror. Thick but nimble fingers traced arcane patterns on the silvery surface.

"Shaykosch!" the waterhorse wizard bellowed, his large face now drenched with a red sweat that matched his robes. "Face me, Beast!"

The Gray Wolf spun away from his gluttonous hilltop feast, scattering the swordsmen mounting the hill. He caught the flash of Hipparcos' mirror and snarled through his sticky purple muzzle. "I remember these parallax tricks, hippopotamus. Where is your piggy proctor? I would like to meet him for my next meal."

Ignoring the barbs, Hipparcos tilted his mirror to catch the Wolf's corrupt reflection and traced a quick ring around each of the Wolf's legs. A glowing shackle appeared on each of Shaykosch's actual legs attached to a glowing chain that disappeared into the paw-churned ground. The grassy hill rippled with the force of Shaykosch's tests against his new restraints.

"Not nearly as good as the other Mirror Mages I have encountered, hippopotamus. Your spell is weak. Let me show you." With a savage barrel roll, the Wolf wrenched loose of the shackles on his left legs and bowled to the bottom of the hill, snapping all of the glowing chains. He confidently landed upright and ready for battle. Grass, splintered wood, and cotton candy sticks spiked from the Wolf's fur like a child's drawing of a porcupine. The magical shackles and chains were gone.

"I am still hungry, so I am done with you, mage." Shaykosch inhaled an uncanny amount of air and then blew it directly at Hipparcos. Despite his girth, the fetid blast of breath spun Hipparcos around like a top, slamming him into the cart-mounted pipe organ. It tipped over in an unholy cacophony of clanging metal pipes, splintering wood, and yelling hippopotamus. The Wolf's mighty breath also encouraged the flames of the Z'more pits to reach out and lick the nearest tablecloths, setting them ablaze.

As the Deathless One took a moment to shake the accumulated debris from his fur like a wet dog, King Quellabaum dove from the smoke-filled sky armed with a booth sign liberated en route. He launched his ersatz missile at the Wolf, and then pulled out of his peregrine dive with a practiced loop-the-loop maneuver. The wooden plank speared Shaykosch through his left side, momentarily pinning him to the ground.

With powerful flaps, the winged Monkey King hovered over the Wolf. "Heh. Looky dere." Quellabaum grinned around his cigar at the painted sign he had randomly plucked. "I 'Salve-d the Day', all right."

Hipparcos came to in a pile of musical and marshmallow debris and stared into the smoky Zo sky. Now what? Those shackles should have easily held the Wolf long enough to muster additional forces. Apparently the Three Troll Test for binding spells needed to be reworked. Maybe a Moochy Hexadrome? No. Too long. A Boreal Core? No, the Wolf would likely turn any wind to his advantage. A Quadrivial ... his train of thought was rudely interrupted by a greenfleece sheep tearing a chunk from Hipparcos' already ragged robe, testing it for edibility. That was it! Hipparcos bolted upright, somehow startling a sheep that had assumed a battleground was a suitable place to graze.

Hipparcos disentangled himself from the remains of the pipe organ cart and stood up. Fortunately his mirror's protections had withstood the Wolf's battering – it gleamed at him from the ground nearby. He scooped it up, blew the dust from its silvery surface, and angled it to catch the counterpart Jamboree.

With deliberate gestures on top of the reflection, he quickly shepherded a mix of items to him from the picnickers' abandoned articles: steel wool from Van Lief's vest pocket, a clump of green wool from the battlefield-indifferent female sheep (still chewing on his scrape of robe), a fluffy morphing cloud from above the field, and Imperial Minister Jellia's sea wool scarf woven from the filaments with which the giant Rosson clams attach themselves to the sea floor. The items flocked towards his mirror and spun lazily in front the hippo's prodigious belly.

Shaykosch sensed the magicks forming again and twisted his body to snap the wooden plank pinning him to the ground. With an enraged snarl and a bottlebrush tail clearly signaling his bloody intentions, he rolled into a spring loaded crouch to face Hipparcos.

Hipparcos returned the Deathless One's angry gaze. "Wolf! You must know that the whole purpose of our Order is to defeat you at every turn. We will always have more than one way to stop your savagery. If you think your disguise so clever today, then a wolf in sheep's clothing you shall truly be!" The mage gripped his mirror tighter and incanted:

> *Ram of fire and Ewe of earth.*
> *Wether of aether and Sheep sea-berthed.*
> *Begone! Declawed! A wolf no more!*
> *I shear you from this mortal shore!*
>
> *Take my taste of all things sweet*
> *To change the Gray Wind's howl to bleat.*
> *No hands shall knit this Wolfen fleece*
> *Or else uncomb Zo's worsted peace!*

The spell crackled about the beast's fur needling him like a thousand angry fleas. He growled and snapped at the magicks, ears back and hackles raised. The sparkling points haloed into four rings each looping a lupine leg again before the giant gray wolf could leap free. Shaykosch violently contorted himself. Finding his shape-shifting ability blocked, his rage shook the clouds.

Without losing contact with the mirrored surface, Hipparcos reclipped his mirror to his belt, and left one hand firmly on his mirror. He ushered the odd items towards the top of the hill with his free hand, and an elemental flock member arced neatly into each of the Wolf's magical shackles. Sensing the spell's coda, the Gray Wind roared, "Know this, Hipparcos! It will not be my tail you see next time. It will be my fangs!"

With a final sweeping gesture that spread his arms wide, Hipparcos quartered Shaykosch before the Zolanders' very eyes. The four bloodless parts took on a sheep-like shape, shimmered, and vortexed from the hilltop into his mirrored buckle. Hipparcos staggered backward, and both the mirrored glass and the inscribed belt plate housing it shattered into a thousand shiny splinters.

Hipparcos recovered his balance and faced the amazed Jade City swordsmen and Indigon Infantry that had replaced the long-gone picnickers on the field, advising them: "Master Hogg warned us this day would come again. Do not think The Deathless Wolf is gone. He will doubtless return when we least expect, for his hunger is endless. May the heroes among you be prepared!" He bent to begin collecting the shattered mirror and promptly collapsed from exhaustion, face first into a crumpled stack of Azulberry pies that he would no longer be able to taste.

* * *

A few days later, the Grassy Field had been mostly cleared and restored, except where the Wolf King's pads and hot desert breath had gnashed the land. A messenger had been dispatched to the diamond anthills of the crystalline Adamants to see if Old Stinky Gaster's colony was still available to heal the soil. Injuries were tended to and travelers returned home regaling all they met with the news of Shaykosch's menace and defeat. Hipparcos was fêted as a hero, and he was said to have had an audience with the Zorcerer Himself/Herself/Itself, but as with most dealings with the Zorcerer, there is no certain record of the event.

Regardless of the number of Zolanders who witnessed the Wolf's dramatic capture and punishment that semi-Windsday on the Grassy Field, the Roly-Poly Prince continued to proclaim (when it best suited his peacock pride – which was often) that it was the Giallon muffins that had saved the empire from The Hunger of the Deathless Wolf. But thanks to Hipparcos and the Order of the Mirror, there were many more Grassy Field Bubble Picnic and Goodtime Marshmallow Jamborees to be had.

Oh, and belatedly, the Violan honey won the Rainbow Ribbon that year.

THE END

The Gingerbread Knight

by Chad Underkoffler

Once Upon A Time, in the Land of Zo. . .

There was a kingdom called Viola, high in the northern mountains. It was a magical land – even more magical than the rest of Zo! – chock full of witches, goblins, Talking Animals, Living Toys, winged monkeys, dragons, and all other sorts of strange and wonderful creatures.

Up in Mystery Valley, between the villages of Warlock Dock and Whistlefree, there was a misty wood. In this forest, along the Oaken Road, was the Gingerbread cottage of Goodwife Sweetinbargendol. Everybody just called her "Goody Sweet" to save time. She was a witch.

Now, Goody Sweet lived up to her name: she was a nice witch. She made her magic for the benefit of the nearby villagers and other residents of Mystery Valley. She taught the cubs and kits of some of the Talking Animals their letters and sums. She brokered the peace between the tribes of Dusk Goblins and Dawn Goblins that haunted the ridges around the valley. She kept the Oaken

Road safe and pleasant with her spells. And once a year, for the Midwinter Festival, she made magical treats for everyone: cakes that played music, pies that floated like balloons, candies that glowed in the dark. (Some even say she's the reason the Windy Gap Dragon stopped eating Farmer Franklin's sheep!) Everyone in Mystery Valley loved – or at least respected – Goody Sweet.

That is why, one day, she had an unexpected visitor: the King Bee of Castle Hive.

The bees of Castle Hive take the nectar of the Strange Violets that grow on Razor Peak and produce a charmed honey of a pale purple hue. At the time of this tale, Goody Sweet was one of the King Bee's best customers, trading spells, advice, or a jug of molasses from Rosso in the far south for a tiny crock of the violet honey, for it was powerful magic.

So, when the King Bee appeared on her doorstep, bedraggled, alone, without any attendant apiary knights or in the company of any of his beautiful daughters, and bearing no crocks of charmed honey, Goody Sweet was worried. "What is wrong, Your Majesty?" she asked as she brought him inside and sprinkled some brown sugar into a saucer to restore him.

"Castle Hive has been attacked!" the Bee gasped. "My apiary knights are all slain, my castle despoiled, my daughters buzzing piteously in the wilderness! A group of brigands came out of nowhere, with no warning, and broke down our walls to steal our purple riches! I come to beg for your aid, Goody Sweet. Can you help us?"

The witch nodded, dusted off her hands, and tied on her special apron. "Let's see what we can cook up for you, King Bee."

In her kitchen of wonders, Goody Sweet creamed together butter and sugar, added a dollop of dark molasses, cracked in a wyvern's egg, cut in lard from Annwyn's pigs, and sifted together baking powder, flour, salt, and cinnamon. The she added a dash of vinegar, a precious drop or two of the violet honey itself, and a heavy pinch of ground Thunderbolt Root – the strongest ginger in all of Zo, which only grows in dirt that has been struck by lightning.

As she whispered hard secrets and hidden truths to the dough, she rolled it out thin and flat. Then, with her silver knife, she cut out a man-shaped figure in thirteen elegant, curving strokes. Goody Sweet placed it daintily upon a floured baking stone, and slid the whole into her red-hot oven to cook.

When the gingerbread man came out, she decorated him deftly. His eyes were chunks of candied cherry atop sweet raisins, his eyebrows and lips were of royal icing (in purple and blue), and two gumdrops served as buttons. As the cookie cooled, he began to stir and awaken.

Goody Sweet said to King Bee, "Here is a Living Confection warrior strong enough to save your people and bring your enemies to justice."

Despite his faith in Goody Sweet's magic, the King Bee looked skeptical. "But there's just one of him, and he's just a cookie."

Suddenly, there was a flash, the gingerbread man was gone from the cooling rack, and the table upon which the King Bee stood lifted high into the air! The King Bee fell to his knees (well, to four of his knees), and looked down over the edge. There below, lifting up the entire table by one of its legs, stood the gingerbread man... and all this with a single mitten-like hand!

The Living Confection put the table back down (gently), then leapt up (easily) to tower over the King Bee (threateningly). "Your Majesty, I am strong and fast and nimble and smart – more than a match for any villains of art. I will serve you, in a manner true blue."

The King Bee looked from cookie to witch, who nodded in

agreement. "He will," said Goody Sweet simply.

The King Bee shrugged his shoulders (well, four of them) and said, "So be it." Looking up at the cookie, he said, mustering what imperiousness he could, "Kneel before me."

The orders of a King, even if he be a Bee, are not to be taken lightly, so the cookie knelt. The King Bee lifted up a nearby candy cane with his arms (well, four of them), and tapped the Living Confection once on each of his crusty shoulders. "I dub thee the Gingerbread Knight. Arise, and go forth to subdue my enemies."

The Gingerbread Knight stood, and took the candy cane from the King. He quickly fashioned himself a helmet out of a sagging macaroon and a shield out of a stale donut. Then, bowing to the King Bee and Goody Sweet, he leapt down from the table and ran across the floor lickety-split, out the door and down the Oaken Road in a twinkle. As the new-made knight loped along the path at remarkable speed, he had only one destination: Castle Hive.

*   *   *

The Gingerbread Knight ran like the wind, and in a shorter time than would be expected, he arrived at the wreckage of Castle Hive. The buttresses and walls and ramparts of wax lay broken and melted upon the grassy sward. Worse still, the bodies of the valiant apiary knights speckled the green like drops of molten gold.

The Living Confection's cherry eyes blinked, then narrowed, then picked out the trail of the brigands who had shattered the castle and its protectors. Along their path were broken combs leaking the rare violet honey into the dust. The Knight was angered by this waste of a precious thing, and leapt onto the trail, anger lending even more speed to his gingerbread legs.

Soon, he came upon the first villain: a human man, pushing a wheelbarrow full of crocks of violet honey. He quickly darted in front of the brigand, planted his stubby feet into the dust of the trail, and cried out loudly:

Ho there, varlet!

Stand and fight.

You can't beat me –

I'm the Gingerbread Knight!

The man just laughed, and set down his ill-gotten burden. Taking a heavy maul from the wheelbarrow, he advanced upon the Gingerbread Knight. "I am going to smash you into pieces, cookie, and eat you with my tea."

With a flash of red and white, the Knight's candy cane parried the maul once, twice, thrice! Then the Knight leapt high into the air, and pummeled the brigand about the head until the villain fell unconscious from his wounds – for the Gingerbread Knight was far, far, far stronger than one would think a cookie the size of a child's palm could be. Using some licorice whips, the Knight bound the brigand for the King Bee's justice, and then returned to his hunt.

*   *   *

Over hill and dale ran the Gingerbread Knight. The trail zipped away under his pumping legs like ribbon candy. In a wink, he came upon a second brigand: a Talking Goat, who held three of the King Bee's beautiful daughters captive in a net on a stick. The Princess Bees wailed in their delicate buzzing voices, but the Goat sneered at them and made vulgar suggestions.

The Knight ran straight up the trunk of a nearby tree and leapt branch to branch, in order to get farther ahead. Then, he dropped down before the Goat and his captives, like a brown thunderbolt from heaven. Clashing his candy cane against his donut shield, he shouted:

> *Ho there, varlet!*
>
> *Stand and fight.*
>
> *You can't beat me –*
>
> *I'm the Gingerbread Knight!*

"You tiny piece of flour and sugar – you think you can best me?!" and the Goat threw the netted Princesses to the side of the trail. He then lowered his horns and charged the Knight, hoping to smash him into crumbs.

With great nimbleness, the Knight danced aside at the last moment, and hooked the villain's ankle with the crook of his weapon. As the Goat started to trip and fall and sprawl, the Gingerbread Knight struck his behind with his donut shield, putting his not inconsiderable strength behind the strike.

The force of the Knight's blow sent the Goat flying through the air at great speed. Eventually, a tree blocked his flight path. The Goat rammed into it, horns first! Sunk six inches deep into the wood, they held him there fast. He bleated in rage as the Gingerbread Knight freed his prisoners.

The Princess Bees all kissed their rescuer – then kissed him again, for he was both sweet and spicy – before he sent them back to the safety of Goody Sweet's cottage. Their royal father would come for the Goat in time, to serve him for his crimes, but the Gingerbread Knight had no time to linger. He ran on, hot after the other brigands.

*   *   *

On and on the tireless Living Confection ran. Steep hills and fallen trees were nothing to him. He leapt over wide gullies without reducing his speed. The villains were escaping with their booty, to whatever hidey-holes were available to them. Speed was of the essence.

Suddenly, on the banks of the river Wozzle, the Knight came upon another brigand: a Bear, hefting two gigantic combs of the precious violet honey. The river behind the villain sparked and burbled, rushing wide with meltwater from the mountains of Razor Peak and Thunderhome. The mud along the banks on both sides was pristine, telling of flash-flooding within the last week.

The Gingerbread Knight ran up to the Bear and kicked him in the tail before giving his battle cry:

> Ho there, varlet!
>
> Stand and fight.
>
> You can't beat me –
>
> I'm the Gingerbread Knight!

While the bear stumbled, he did not fall, being both massive and thick-hided. He turned slowly, spied the cookie, and set down the heavy combs roughly. Only then did he growl at the Knight, "You are nothing! Smaller than the salmon I smack out of the river every day to consume. I will crush you into crumbs, and let the wind blow you away."

The Gingerbread Knight simply lifted his candy cane.

With surprising speed in one so huge, the bear leapt forward – and the battle was on!

Immense paw struck against donut shield, razor claws striking sparks from sprinkles. Candy cane bounced off of stone bear skull to no effect. Teeth of ivory yellow snapped off an edge of macaroon helm. Cookie fist met furry jowl. It was an epic duel.

Still, the might of the Bear was no match for the prowess of the Gingerbread Knight. Slowly, the Knight was gaining, pushing the ursine brigand back, back, back towards the river. Fear blossomed in the villain's eyes, for he knew his end was near.

Just then a crimson flash came between the Knight and his foe. It was a one-eyed Fox, who ripped out the Bear's throat neatly with his fangs! Landing neatly on his back-socked hands, the Fox lashed out with his feet, kicking the brigand into the rushing waters of the Wozzle!

*　　*　　*

The Gingerbread Knight leapt back, cane and shield at the ready, prepared to deal with this new – and obviously dangerous – threat.

But the Fox turned to him and bowed, saying, "Pardon me, Sir Knight, for interrupting, but I had a score to settle with these brigands and their leader, just as you seem to." The Fox completed his bow, and adjusted his eyepatch before continuing. "I am Festius, a neighbor of King Bee. When I returned from my morning constitutional, I discovered the chaos these villains had caused, and began tracking their leader. For, does the proverb not say, 'Remove the head, and the body will wander around bumping into things until it falls down'?"

The Knight relaxed at these words slightly. "I thank you then, Festius, for your aid in slaying that Bear, the leader of the brigand band."

Festius laughed. "Oh no no no, Sir Knight, that furry lummox was in no wise the leader of these varlets. The leader – a brilliant and deadly sort – has already crossed the Wozzle. This I know from my nose," he tapped his whitened muzzle, "which has never failed me, and my eye, which saw the villain cross not a quarter hour past before you arrived." The Fox pointed across the river towards the smooth mud of the far bank. "I could help you bring him to the justice he so richly deserves."

One of the Gingerbread Knight's purple eyebrows quirked at this, and he said slowly and deliberately, "And how would you aid me in this quest?"

"Well, firstly, you see that the Wozzle is running fast and high. It is too deep to ford and the nearest bridge is leagues away."

The Knight nodded. "Go on."

"You are a doughty bit of biscuit, Sir Knight, but your nature is susceptible to moisture. For if you tried to swim the river, would you not get soggy and break into pieces in the current?"

"Your words may be true, Festius. What of it?"

The Fox bowed again. "It would be an honor to swim the Wozzle, bearing you safe and dry upon my back. Then we can together track and chase the leader of these foul brigands."

The Gingerbread Knight pondered a moment, cherry eyes flickering over the river, the Fox, the bank. Then, he nodded, and leapt onto Festius' back, where he stood, waiting.

"Excellent, Sir Knight," chuckled the Fox, once he got over his surprise at the Living Confection's alacrity. He walked down the untouched mud of the riverbank and waded into the Wozzle.

About a quarter of the way across the river, water started lapping up Festius' back and around the Knight's feet. "Climb up onto my neck, "said the Fox, "since the waters have risen."

"As you say," replied the Gingerbread Knight, and climbed higher.

About halfway across the Wozzle, the water had reached the Fox's neckline as he swam. "Climb onto my head," said Festius, "since the waters have risen again."

"As you say," replied the Gingerbread Knight, and climbed even higher.

About three-quarters of the way across, Festius stopped swimming. He gave a barking laugh before saying, "And now, Sir Knight, since you have nowhere to go, I shall *eat you*!" Then the Fox tossed his head in such a way as to send the Gingerbread Knight tumbling right into his mouth!

Yet all was not lost – quick as lightning the Knight jammed his donut shield between the Fox's jaws, holding them open just long enough to swing back onto Festius' muzzle. There the Gingerbread Knight crouched, his cherry eyes burning, staring into the one living eye of the Fox.

"I was prepared for your treachery, Fox, for *you* are the leader of the brigands who sacked Castle Hive."

"How – ack! – did you – ptooie! – know?" spluttered Festius around a mouthful of stale donut.

"There were no tracks in the mud leading down the riverbank, nor were there tracks up across the opposite side. And if a flash flood had thundered down the Wozzle in the last fifteen minutes, it would have been audible for leagues around." The Knight raised his candy cane for a mighty blow. "And now you die, villain."

"You will die, too!" protested the Fox. "A soggy death in the Wozzle awaits you if you kill me now!"

The Gingerbread Knight nodded grimly. "So be it." And then he struck, burying his weapon to the crook into the Fox's skull, killing him instantly.

As the Fox sank beneath the waters of the Wozzle, the Knight felt those waters saturating his feet and legs, making them soft and soggy. "The villains have been brought to justice, one way or another," he thought to himself, "and justice is enough for me."

At that point the Wozzle closed over his head, yet strangely he did not ensoggify and break apart. . . but that's another tale.

THE END

Little Jack and the Yellow Dress

By Michael Hill

Once Upon A Time, in the Land of Zo...

Little Jack was the carpenter's son in the village of Flinsk – a speck amid the boundless, grassy plains of Giallo – and he was a good boy. He grew up thoughtful and strong, and followed his father, Big Jack, in those ways and every other. Indeed, he became so skilled that he earned a few pennies now and again for extra work he performed for the other villagers after the end of a long day toiling for his father, and shortly before his twelfth birthday, he found he'd accumulated quite a few!

As the days grew shorter and harvest approached, Little Jack formulated a plan. For weeks, he redoubled his efforts to keep his father's workshop immaculate, to perform every task with the utmost care and skill. Every cut he made was straight, every nail sunk even with the surface, every edge sanded to silky perfection.

So it was when he asked permission to accompany his father to the large town of Violinsk, Big Jack granted it with smiling pride and a tousling of Little Jack's curly blond hair, bidding his son to harness the family ox. So Little Jack and Big Jack loaded up the family wagon with tables and desks, cabinets and chairs, and with Little Jack's grandfather – Old Jack, naturally – they rode in style to the town of Violinsk, a place with cobbled streets and gates and taxes and nearly two thousand souls!

When they arrived, Little Jack dutifully stabled the ox, then – while Big Jack and Old Jack took care of business – he set about the market square, eyes sharp and ever-alert for the perfect gift, a work of beauty to match his vision of the sweet Alfira, a girl of the village who was about his own age. But he met with frustration, time and again: The jewelers wanted a fortune for anything decent; the silversmith's wares were outright disappointing; and he rejected the blacksmith and sundry vendors as unsuitable. In the end, after every other option proved fruitless, Little Jack cautiously made his way into the dress-maker's stall.

He felt a little embarassed, like a trespasser on forbidden ground. For reasons even he could not explain, Little Jack felt as if he would be caught and die of embarassment at any moment. He nearly lost his nerve when he heard a kind, soothing voice.

"May I help you, kind sir?" asked the booth's proprietor, a well-rounded woman of middle age whose dress – especially the bodice – was a marvel of structural engineering and no small feat of modesty, all at once. Little Jack's mouth felt dry – he wasn't really sure when that started – but he managed to get out an answer without his voice cracking.

"I'm looking for a dress, for a... for a...." he said, a warm flush on his cheeks prompting him to drop his gaze to the floor and trail off.

"For a lady friend?" prompted the proprietor, favoring him with a wide, friendly smile that was only slightly condescending.

"Yes! For a lady friend!" he blurted out, louder than he'd intended, but the dress-maker only softened her smile further.

"It's a surprise," he added, somewhat more quietly.

On closer inspection, the woman seemed less imposing. Her cheeks were round and rosy, her smile quick and sincere up to the crinkles around her warm, brown eyes. In retrospect, Little Jack was only surprised that there wasn't a tray of cooling cookies somewhere about. He grinned at his own foundless fear.

"Oh, dear, yes, a surprise! How wonderful! Now, tell your Auntie May a little bit about her, maybe I'll have a suggestion for you," she offered.

"Well, ah…" Little Jack felt as if he were on the verge of stammering, so he clamped his mouth shut instead, and furrowed his brow. He'd never considered quantifying what was important about her, so for him, this was uncharted territory.

When he managed to open his mouth, a little puff of breath came out before he spoke.

"She's about my age. Her father's a shepherd. Her mother's an embroiderer. So she works a lot in wool," he said.

"I was rather thinking you'd tell me about her hair and eyes, and how tall she is and about her general shape," she said, with the slightest glint of mischief in her expression.

So Jack explained Alfira's beautiful hair; her astonishingly blue eyes; her clear, creamy skin; the fact that she was an inch shorter than he; and then sort of petered out as he ran out of things he felt comfortable thinking about, let alone saying aloud to a stranger. Fortunately, he appeared to have said enough.

"I have just the thing!" the shop-keeper practically cooed with delight as she turned to a chest on her right, and retrieved a bright yellow dress that fairly shone where the sun caught its smooth, soft surface. The bodice was trimmed with white lace in a pattern of interlocking doves and hearts, and the apron of the dress was embroidered with the same theme.

"It's made from the finest weave…" Auntie May began, but she saw Little Jack's expression and let her voice trail off.

The yellow dress was the second most beautiful thing Little Jack had seen in his entire life, and he was immediately taken by thoughts of Alfira, her long, coppery tresses against the sharp yellow of the dress. With surprisingly little haggling, Little Jack posessed himself of the dress, wrapped in a burlap package for travelling, and spent nearly every penny he'd saved.

In truth, Little Jack would have offered every coin in his pocket for the dress, but everyone knew that only a fool spent all his money in one place, and he'd decided – wisely – not to be that sort of fool.

For this was his plan: He would present the beautiful Alfira with both the dress and his invitation to the Harvest Dance. Surely, in combination, the two would be successful, or so Little Jack thought, as he nervously sweated over the plans each night when he lay down to sleep.

When he thought of Alfira, it felt as if someone had taken out his heart and replaced it with a different model, just a half-size too big, too loud. The feeling had been building for awhile, and he'd wondered about it at first, unsure why the neighbor girl suddenly seemed so much more interesting, but without so much as a by-your-leave, it had grown beyond his ability to reason with.

The ride home to the little village of Flinsk seemed to Little Jack as if it lasted forever. Each turn and stretch of road seemed twice as long, thrice as long, seven times as long as it had before. His thoughts turned to the lovely Alfira: Her limpid blue eyes, her long, copper-gold hair, her radiant skin, and most of all, her lovely voice, so enchanting when filled with laughter and light!

And yet, he feared deeply her scorn. He had heard her mock her younger brother, and he remembered the chill in his veins. Perhaps she thought he was an oaf! Maybe she'd mistaken his humble and bumbling silence for stupidity! What if she feared his rough, calloused hands' touch against her – it must be presumed – delicate, creamy complexion?

By the time Little Jack returned to the village, bouncing away on the buckboard of his father's wagon, he was so eager and afraid and full of excitement that he leapt right down, dress in hand, and dashed straight away to the small house where Alfira lived with her parents, leaving Big Jack and Old Jack to put away the ox and cart.

But as he ran, the bright reflection of the sun shone against the yellow dress, and caught the attention of the village witch who, roused from her contemplations on the unfair nature of life, cast her keen, hawklike gaze upon Little Jack and his task. She turned her hooded gaze to the street, the tip of her long, twisted nose wriggling in distaste, one ancient, calcified lip lifting into a primal sneer.

Grudmilla, the old woman, was a gruesome hag, her flesh puffy with age, wrinkles deep as ditches. Her eyes were sharp, though the left one was twice the size of the right, the gaze from beneath her drooping lids was dark with malice, and dull as tarnished metal. Her hair writhed downward from her head in filthy, time-worn locks; and her thick, chipped yellow nails bit into her fingers as she watched the yellow dress flicker by in Little Jack's draft.

She ran the tip of her wart-infested tongue over her cracked, pale lips. She was a creature of hate, and she'd had a lot of practice at it, so she'd become quite skilled with its theory and application. In Little Jack's stride and the fluttering of the pretty dress, she detected that True Love was afoot.

She nodded solemnly, though she was alone, and readied herself. In her apron pocket was a dead, black bird, and Grudmilla lovingly stroked its soured corpse as she began a whispered incantation.

Little Jack pounded upon Alfira's door, and was rewarded when she, herself, opened it! He opened his mouth to speak.

"Alfira," he said, then closed his mouth resolutely. He'd felt a stammer coming on, and that just couldn't do. He swallowed and dared to look up into her quizzical blue eyes, a tease of a smile playing along the edges of her mouth.

Oh, please, he prayed, *please let it be lighthearted if she laughs.* He'd never had a chance to practice asking a girl to a dance, and part of him was sure she would laugh at his impudence. Even now, it whispered that he might not be good enough for her, but with a bit of effort and faith, he brushed his fears aside.

"I've got this dress, and I was hoping you'd wear it to the Harvest Dance. With me," he said, a bit less skillfully than he'd planned.

With a squeal, Alfira leaned forward and gave him a big squeeze. Then she took the dress from his trembling grasp and held it against her bodice for measure.

She'd been waiting for a bit over a year for Little Jack to come to his senses, and excitement coursed along her every nerve.

Then the little hairs on the back of her neck and arms stood up, and her mind raced to put every fact precisely into place. For nine generations unto nine generations, the women in her family had been cursed to forever have True Love denied. Her mother and grandmother had refused to speak in detail of their own experiences, but Alfira had gathered this much:

Eighteen generations ago, a particularly beauteous ancestor of Alfira's became involved in a love triangle with the man of her dreams and, regrettably, a sorceress of no small power. When the sorceress' lover scorned her, she placed a powerful magic curse on the poor woman and her female descendants, that True Love would be as fickle and fleeting for them as it had proven for the sorceress, herself.

Alfira didn't like the sound of that, so she had thought up some ideas of her own. She planned ahead, and in a knapsack next to her bed rested a kit containing everything she'd ever thought might help: raw salt, garlic, wolvesbane, a hammer and stake, a long knife – everything she might need short of a magic sword, which she'd been unable to obtain.

"Yes!" she said, loudly at first, then, after a furtive glance, more quietly, her gaze locked on his. "Yes. But there's something I have to go get. Right now."

Little Jack's world was swirling. In all his imaginings, he'd rarely allowed himself to ponder the sweetness of that one little word, "Yes!" and he felt as if he were over-full of the most wondrous stuff! His heart was throbbing, his blood pumping, his body felt heavier than the earth and lighter than a feather. For one long moment, he even forgot to breathe.

But no sooner were the words spoken when suddenly, from the sky, a great black bird swooped down! In one great claw it snatched Alfira – dress and all – from the ground and stuffed her into a bag that hung by a rope from its waist. The bird took to the air with a great cackling caw, a ripping screech full of envy and triumph, leaving the astounded Little Jack in slack-jawed contemplation of the empty space where once the fair and charming Alfira stood.

Alfira wasted little time lamenting her well-laid plans; her emergency bag was beyond her reach – no matter. After a few moments of shock – the witch had made her move with admirable decision – Alfira made a quick inventory of her resources. She felt around inside the sack and discovered a number of fist-shaped oval objects – stones, she thought, surely – and stuck her hands into her pockets to discover what she might have.

"Ouch!" she cried, pulling the left hand from her apron pocket. Her palm had been pierced by a single, long, iron needle, which she immediately pulled out. As she sucked at the drop of blood that welled up from her palm, she got an idea, and quick as a flash, the idea became a plan.

Far below, Little Jack stood, rubbing his jaw, turning as the shadow of the bird passed over his body and watching it bear away the sack containing both his hard-won companion and her hard-earned dress. The tragic unfairness of the situation threatened to overwhelm Little Jack, whose insecurities had prepared him for a hundred travails, but not this one.

Then he pushed his fears away, into the back of his mind, to be dealt with another day, and allowed himself to be struck fully by the need to act swiftly, just as surely as the needle Alfira dropped bounced right off the top of his head!

Inside the bag, Alfira gritted her teeth in frustration, and tore at the seam with her hands.

Already she could see Little Jack and the houses of Flinsk getting smaller and smaller. Escape was impossible. She closed her eyes for a second to steady herself, lost between the odd beauty of the bird's eye view and the abiding desire to vomit.

Little Jack looked up, just in time to see a small oval shadow fall from the retreating silhouette of the bird.

Without another thought, Little Jack broke into a run, chasing the black bird silhouetted against the bright blue sky, its wings flapping ponderously as it struggled to make its escape. He saw a small oval shadow fall from the monstrous bird to the ground and, for a fleeting moment, he was alive with the fear that Alfira had been dropped. He clenched his jaw and ran on, huffing and puffing.

Soon, Little Jack was sweating, muscles aching, when he reached the fallen object – an egg – sitting square in the middle of the road. And what an egg! Its surface was crossed with wires of precious metal, and the entire rounded oval was inlaid with pearls and rubies and every sort of precious jewel!

Even the richest citizens of Violinsk had never seen such marvels! To own, to sell one such egg would make not just a person, but an entire family wealthy! Each was a treasure worthy of a king!

The egg was so beautiful that Little Jack stared for a few long, slow moments, his eyes tracing the lines and curves, caressing the facets of the many-colored gems. Then Little Jack saw a crack spreading across its surface. He brought the egg up to his ear and listened carefully. Inside, he heard a plaintive chirping.

His lips frowned lightly at the corners, and his brow furrowed in the middle. It seemed a shame to wreck further destruction upon such beauty, but inside was a living thing, struggling to make its way free into the world.

Little Jack thrust his fingers into the crack and pried apart the egg to reveal a tiny green bird, which let out a joyful cry, and hopped out its shell onto his fingertip. It peered up at him with wide, adoring eyes then performed a dainty curtsey, if Little Jack's eyes weren't mistaken.

The bird whistled a few happy notes, then flew off, circling Little Jack several times, as if in salute, before heading due east. Little Jack marvelled at the flight of the little bird, his hand over his eyes to shade them from the sun, and it was then that he saw the second egg fall from the receding form of the great, black monster bearing the burlap sack that contained Alfira.

He knelt for a moment to gather up the scraps of precious metal and gems that remained, shoved them into his pockets and ran with determination, cheeks bulging, chest heaving from the effort, faster and faster – even faster than before! He'd never thought himself much of a runner, but to Little Jack, it felt as if a gentle breeze were pressing every so lightly against his back, and the sensation strengthened his resolve.

Soon, Little Jack found the second egg, like the first, laying in the middle of the road. This time, the crack was a little wider, the bird – which was blue – made a deep bow over Jack's outstretched finger, sang a few happy notes and launched itself into the sky.

Little Jack ran. More eggs fell, and Little Jack cracked each one open. The birds sang their worshipful gratitude as he set them free, each and every one: green and blue, red and brown, black and white, purple and orange, and finally, a little yellow bird – the ninth, in all – which tweeted its cheerful little song and hopped right onto Little Jack's shoulder! And with each egg, Little Jack felt the wind at his back more keenly.

This could only be an omen of good luck, Little Jack thought – each of the other birds had flown off in a different direction, east, south, west, north and the points midway in between – but the tiny yellow bird held tight as he sped down the road, as fast as his legs could carry him.

Grudmilla – for it was she who had transformed herself into a great bird – stood next to a large bag with a small hole in it. She was rapidly running out of steam, so she had glided to a stop along the road. She cocked her head to the side. Something was wrong with the bag. It didn't used to have a hole.

With an outraged squawk, she took the end of the bag in her sharp beak and upended it upon the ground, revealing Alfira as the only remaining treasure within the coarse bag. The witch, neither inexperienced nor foolish, quickly realized what must have happened, and returned herself to human form amid tendrils of dark smoke that wisped away into the breeze.

Centuries of toiling over the bubbling cauldron, of hunching over foul tomes at midnight and digging for corpses had taken its toll on the wizened hag. She definitely wasn't as young as she'd used to be, she decided, and it was high time she made a pact with darkness to ensure renewed vigor.

Perhaps she'd start stealing both youth and beauty from that awful family she'd been tormenting for centuries. Alfira, that was the name of their latest girl. Or maybe she'd restore her own youth with the stuff of their very souls! Yes. Yes. Yes, that was the one she'd pick, if she had the chance. Delicious.

But that was a plan for the future. In the here and now, the fool girl had thrown away her precious eggs!

"Bread crumbs," she muttered under her breath as she advanced upon Alfira. Her voice began to rise with rage and disbelief. "You used my most precious treasures for bread crumbs!"

Grudmilla paused and gathered her wits with a slow, deep breath, then released it with a raspy chuckle.

"Well, don't you worry, my pretty little one. Your boyfriend will be here soon, and I'll take my 'bread crumbs' back from his corpse if I have to. And probably even if I don't."

"Never!" cried Alfira. "No one can stop True Love!"

The witch leaned back her head and let loose a laugh, a hollow, empty laugh filled at once with grandeur and solitude.

"Yes, yes," Grudmilla said, a sly smile working from one corner of her mouth to the other and back again. "That's what they say. That's what they *all* say!"

Alfira went pale.

"So your mother said, before I gave her lover a giant rat's head."

Alfira glared upward at the witch. She wanted to shout "Liar!" at the top of her lungs, but she had a sinking suspicion the witch was telling the truth, and it kept her quiet.

"So your grandmother said, standing over the corpse of her True Love disgustingly dead."

The poor girl's morale was sinking fast. What kind of pride did it take, Alfira wondered, to think she could succeed where seventeen generations of her ancestors had failed? What gall? Yet at the same time, the rising anger within her made her want to leap up and fight, and the witch noticed:

> *Surely your mother told you, child, that love is a lie,*
>> *a service to the self before we die,*
> *We tell ourselves it is pure and strong,*
>> *but its faithfulness is rarely long.*
> *In the end, we are only ambition.*
>> *And "love' is a tool that clouds our vision,*
> *For the meek who cringe at desire,*
>> *for those who fear both shadow and fire.*

The blood coursed loudly in her ears as Alfira balled her hands into fists and forced herself to stay on the ground, listening to Grudmilla's incantation of outrageous blasphemies, of how the witch – this very witch! – had both laid down the curse upon her family and personally seen it through. For the first time, Alfira knew fear, deep and cold and hollow, like a tiny, empty sphere of ice lodged deep in her throat and threatening to expand. Like a frozen seed, the core of fear sent its numbing tendrils outward. She could feel them growing.

Grudmilla recognized the glint of doubt in her eyes, and a leer spread across the wreckage of her withered lips. She stepped closer, leaning down toward Alfira, who would have scrambled away, except she was frozen, paralyzed by fear.

> *You can feel it, deep down inside, can't you, my pretty girl?*
> *The handsome young lad who's the center of your world*
> *May fail you in the end, as your father failed your mother.*
> *You've seen that flame die. You've seen it smothered.*

Alfira closed her eyes and choked back a cry, because everything the witch had said was true. She'd known her parents' True Love had failed, though neither would ever explain how or why or even when, but she saw the sad smiles they exchanged, the rueful glances, the tiniest shake of her mother's head, her father's enduring sense of shame.

> *That love conquers all is just a pretty lie,*
>
> *But you knew that afore – you've got a sharp eye.*

The witch reached down with her gnarled, wizened claw, and made a gentle stroke along the line of Alfira's wet cheek with the soft edge of one fingertip.

She saw the witch's finger coming and resolved not to react, but Alfira shuddered involuntarily, flesh quailing in betrayal of her will.

Grudmilla's voice grew low, mournful, consoling.

> *But much can be made of a girl with a brain.*
>
> *She can be a woman strong, and rule again*
>
> *As our mothers did, in the time before men.*
>
> *I cannot promise you a life without pain.*
>
> *Already, your heart bears its awful strain.*

And, indeed, Alfira could feel its awful grasp spreading, fed by the witch's words. She clenched her jaws and tried hard to focus, to push aside the witch's truths and lies alike, but with each passing second, it got harder and harder to resist their allure.

> *You are better than him. He will do you wrong.*
>
> *He will betray you, because it's you who are strong.*
>
> *And when he finds that out, you'll feel him resent*
>
> *Everything you've ever done for him, and you'll repent.*
>
> *But much can be made of a girl who's so smart.*

Come with me, little sweetling, and we'll go far away

From those mewling wretches and their childish play.

Alfira wept without shame. She felt as if she had confronted a secret, dark truth at the center of the world, and yet…. She had also felt the warm and throbbing glow of her love for Little Jack, and in the incandescent pulse of that vital fuse, she knew hope, and that hope broke through the witch's spell.

"Maybe True Love isn't really destined to win," Alfira said. She dared herself to look the witch right in the eyes and was somewhat surprised when she managed it. "But that just means we have to try hard to make it work. You don't stop embroidering just because you might drop a stitch."

Grudmilla drew back, glaring down at the young, radiant girl in her magnificent dress, and sneered down the length of her crooked nose.

"Then you are as unworthy as all the rest," she croaked.

That was when Little Jack finally caught up to the pair. He stood for a moment, catching his breath, hair astir from wind and effort, staring straight into the wide, glazed eyes of the witch who turned upon Little Jack with the fierceness of a storm rushing across the golden plains.

"You!" Grudmilla cried, her breath a withered whisk of stale, choked air. "You have my eggs! Return them to me, and I will return that which is yours. But I warn you! If you cheat me, I will kill you dead, and grind your bones to make my bread."

Little Jack, who had no better idea in mind, nodded in agreement and stepped forward. He'd always thought that bone bread was a giant's recipe, but now did not seem to be the moment to argue with the homicidal witch who had Alfira trapped.

Right before the witch's eyes, he emptied his pockets, spilling gold and silver thread and sparkling gems across the ground. The witch fell to her knees, running her fingers through the pile of precious ruin, crying out and gnashing her teeth in frustration, holding handfuls of gems and wires up to the light, appraisingly.

"It's not here! It's not here! It's not here!" she shrieked, each time louder than the last. The witch threw a double-handful of wealth to the ground. She rose and pointed a crooked, gnarled finger with a snaggly nail.

"You lied! You lied! And now you'll wish you'd already died!" Grudmilla's howl was wild, full of anguish and desire, like a starving beast about to have its belly filled, and ended with a roiling laughter that sounded like the echoes of mountains crumbling.

"But... but... I gave you everything I have!" Jack shouted.

In desperation, he shoved his hands deep into his pockets, and pulled them the whole way out, until he plucked them from his coat entirely and threw them on the ground! He looked at his hands in disbelief and horror, surely he had nothing left to give!

Then he heard a little chortling whistle. The little yellow bird – still clinging to his shoulder – whispered just a few notes into his ear. And then Little Jack remembered.

He remembered all the birds: green and blue, red and brown, black and white, purple and orange – and yellow! – suddenly each and every tune was clear in his mind, as if renewed by distant echoes from the eight winds. He whistled each of their tunes in turn, grinning as they joined to form a jaunty little melody!

Little Jack was so pleased with himself, he whistled it again, only louder, more smoothly, as he got used to the phrasing. He'd never been much of a whistler – truth be told, he tended to use the gap between his front teeth as much as his actual lips – but today, his breath felt as if it were launching itself from his lungs and out through his lips like a geyser, and his melody poured forth, loud and clear.

The witch screamed, hands held over her ears.

Little Jack stepped forward, still whistling, and the witch drew back from his song! Grudmilla cowered, as if from a mighty thunder, and yelped as if she'd been struck by lightning!

His lips hurt from whistling so hard, so Little Jack made some words to go with his tune and began to sing:

> *I've tamed nine birds from their jewelled cages!*
>
> *I've run faster than the crow flies or a drunkard rages!*
>
> *I'm Little Jack, the carpenter's son!*
>
> *And you'll be dead before I'm done!*

He went straightforth to Alfira, whose enthrallment had been broken by Little Jack's song. He realized, with amazement, that she was wearing the yellow dress!

For just a moment, Little Jack forgot about everything else – the witch, the eggs, the chase – except the lovely Alfira, radiant in his gift. The pair's eyes met and lingered on each other in a way that made the back of Little Jack's neck uncomfortably warm.

He blushed, grinned, dropped his eyes and – for lack of something better to say or do – handed Alfira back the needle she'd dropped as the witch carried her away.

Alfira grew a foxy grin that made Little Jack want to turn and run home again. She strode toward the howling witch, elaborating the song:

> *You may think you've got it in the bag,*
>
> *But now I'm loose, you loathesome hag!*
>
> *With this needle I'll nail you down!*
>
> *I'll kill you, witch, without a frown!*

The witch collapsed in a heaving mass that swore awful curses and sent them howling off in spectral form from her gaping, yellow-toothed maw, incoherent, nearly insensate, smoke trickling from beneath her clothes. (The havoc those curses unleashed. . . is a tale for another time.)

Alfira grabbed the back of the witch's head with one hand, sinking her fingers deep into the shaking mass of greasy hair. She raised the pin high, and Little Jack saw the sun glint off it as she brought it down hard against the hag's staring eye. She shoved hard, but it wasn't enough – the witch was a tough old bird indeed and had closed her time-thickened lids against the very tip of the needle as she howled threats and curses toward the sky – and Little Jack had to help with one final push. But together, they had the strength to force the nail the whole way in.

With one last terrifying howl, the ancient Grudmilla collapsed into a pile of feathers (which swirled away on the breeze) and a mass of snakes (which promptly slithered away into a thick stand of thorny brush) and a volume of inky smoke (that descended into the earth). In the end, all that was left of the witch was a terrible ear-ache for them both, as the echoes of the crone's death-howl grew quiet.

So Alfira and Little Jack gathered up the gems and scraps of metal that were all that remained of the witch's eggs. Alfira put them in her apron pocket, and they walked, home to Flinsk, talking quietly about what the future might hold.

Little Jack seemed confident that the two were about to enter the "happily ever after" stage of their relationship, and Alfira decided that his optimism couldn't hurt, so she spoke not a word against it.

The yellow dress shone in the sun.

Naturally, Little Jack and Alfira both hoped they were done with witches for good. They were wrong. . . but that's another tale for another time.

THE END

The Wooden Pirate

by Chad Underkoffler

Once Upon A Time, in the Land of Zo. . .

There was a kingdom called Rosso, where every year there was held the Crimson Festival, a three-day party where everyone went masked and made merry. Singing, dancing, wooing, and feasting was the business of the day for the festival-goers. Courtiers and commoners mixed and played together in ways unthinkable during the rest of the year. Three days of chaos and fun, where passions ruled.

During one Crimson Festival, during the reign of Bad King Agnemophus, a young ropemaker named Nick Knott spent some of his carefully hoarded savings to acquire the grandest and most realistic costume for the merry-making: the uniform of a Grand Admiral of the Imperial Zo Fleet. Oh, Nick cut a fine figure in his bottle-green coat with brass buttons up the front, the golden braid that spilled across his shoulders and down his arms. His coal-black pants even had a golden stripe that disappeared into the forest-green boots of a naval officer. Under the tall velvet hat

74

bedecked with moa feathers, he wore a simple black domino mask – enough to shield his identity, but not enough to hide his handsome profile.

Nick straightened his back and marched into the riotous streets of Port Carmine from his tiny rooms on Chandler Street. Assuming a commanding air, he felt every inch a maritime hero, even though the sword at his side was nothing more than a wooden hilt painted gold. He sang and danced and drank and listened to stories and told stories and kissed pretty girls and was kissed by pretty girls (and maybe a few boys dressed as girls, nobles dressed as commoners, commoners dressed as nobles, dogs dressed as cats, and vice-versa – no matter, it's the Crimson Festival!) and played cards with a Talking Cat and ate and laughed and had a grand old time, as everyone else was. This was the first Festival he'd attended since his parents died, and he wished to make the most of it.

At a midnight bonfire in Applebottom Square, he bumped into a girl. A girl dressed as an Imperial Soldier, with a uniform much like his, only in lime-green rather than bottle-green, and wearing an enormous avocado green shako. Under her golden domino mask, she had drawn a curling mustache above her lips and a pointy beard upon her chin with lampblack – but neither could cloak her beauty.

"I beg your pardon, Colonel," said Nick, with all the gravity and esprit de corps he could muster. "May I buy you a cup of grog as recompense for my clumsiness?"

The girl held up a half-full wineskin. "No need, Admiral. I have plenty enough to share. Hold out your mug, and Colonel Joy will provide."

He did so, and as the purple wine sloshed into his cup, he introduced himself as "Admiral Nick." Then he said to her, "Shall will military heroes go on a short patrol of the perimeter, in order to protect these citizens of the Empire of Zo and the Kingdom of Rosso?"

Colonel Joy thought this a capital idea, and the pair of them went to investigate a particularly dark and deserted alley. While no enemies of the state were readily apparent, there certainly was a lot of kissing noises. Later, they sang in the streets where Cowtrail meets Threadneedle, ate snow cream cake at the Icehouse, drank spicy mulled cider at the Firefly Tavern, played pitchpenny with a visiting family of Talking Goats from Giallo, and danced around the Roosticon Fountain with a bunch of children who were up far, far, far past their bedtime (but no matter, it's the Crimson Festival!).

As the first rays of sunrise began to gleam above them, the dance ended. Nick and Joy pledged to meet again at dusk on that very spot, to continue their adventures during the festival. Then, they went their separate ways to their separate homes and separate beds, just as everyone else did.

The next night, the sailor met the soldier as agreed, and they spent the whole night having fun. At dawn on the second day, they again parted at the Fountain, promising to meet again when twilight came. As Nick dropped into his narrow bed that morning, he felt something stirring in his chest, but fell asleep before he could identify it.

It came to him the following midnight, on the third and last evening of the Crimson Festival, as he and Joy stood atop the Vermilliad Tower. They had scaled it from the outside because the doors were locked for a private party. As they watched the ships in the harbor of Port Carmine setting off fireworks, Nick took Joy's hand in his, and pledged his love to her. She turned to him, tears in her eyes, and pledged her love to him. They kissed, as flowers of light and thunder surrounded them.

After a long, quiet time, the two drew apart. Joy looked down slightly, and said to Nick, "I believe you, Admiral Nick, but I wonder if you would love me as I am, not as the valiant Colonel Joy."

"I believe I would," said Nick. "I believe I do."

She smiled. "Then let us meet tomorrow, after the Festival has ended, without our costumes and just as we are."

Nick agreed readily.

"Meet me at dusk, in the building on the northwest corner of Threadneedle and Lye Streets," Joy said.

"The laundry?

"Yes."

"I shall."

"Until then, dearest one," said Joy as she scuttled down the tower like a green spider. Nick watched her, his heart beating like a drum in his chest.

At dusk, Nick – now just plain old Nick Knott, rope- and cordmaker – approached the building Joy had designated. The sign read "Hamm Laundry," for that is what it was. Nick stepped inside, where the air was steamy and smelled of soap. Behind a counter stood a Talking Pig wearing a gingham dress and a somewhat soggy wig.

"Are you Mistress Hamm?" asked Nick, smoothing his tunic nervously.

"I am," said Hamm, looking at Nick's lack of laundry to be done, or empty basket or bag. "Picking up or dropping off?"

"Not exactly, ma'am," he said, smiling. "Do you have a human girl named Joy who works here?"

The Pig's eyes narrowed. "I do. What do you want with her?"

"I want her to become my wife. I love her."

Mistress Hamm's eyes widened, then she started to snort. "Oh ho ho! Let's see if you feel the same way in a minute." She shoved her jowly head through the doorway into the laundry rooms. "Joy! Come here! You have a visitor."

Soon, out of a cloud of steam, came a bedraggled and dirty human girl, her dress tattered, her bodice much patched, and her mobcap askew. In bare feet. It was Joy.

Nick laughed and ran to clasp her to his breast. "Hello, Colonel, it's your Admiral."

Joy hugged him in return, but with a look of confusion. "It doesn't matter to you that I am a menial washerwoman? A servant to a Talking Animal? A common nobody?"

"You are certainly somebody. And there's nothing wrong with being common – I am too. What matter?" Nick twirled her around. "I am a ropemaker, common as dirt, but I am free. I have some meager savings, and with what I can get when I sell back my Admiral's uniform to Jack Costumer, I'm sure I can buy your freedom!" He set her down and spun to face the Pig. "What do you say to that, Mistress Hamm? I love this girl, and will place good coin into your trotter to secure her release from indenture."

Mistress Hamm blushed and stuttered, but before she could speak, Joy exclaimed, "You love *me*!" and grabbed Nick by the shoulders, then turned him around into a long, lovely kiss.

Their they stood, locked in love, for a minute, perhaps two, before a rough hand boxed Nick on the ear, separating him from his love and sending him skidding across the flagged floor.

As he tried to get his feet under him, a red boot kicked him across the face. Just as his eyes fluttered and started to roll up into his head, he caught a glimpse of a crimson-red uniform. Before all sounds collapsed into a single dull roar, he heard a gruff man's voice saying, as if from far away, "Really, Princess Joyeux? Embracing a commoner? What will your father say?"

* * *

As Nick swam up out of the darkness into consciousness, he became aware of four things:

One, his head hurt.

Two, his face was smashed against a cold stone floor.

Three, someone was yelling very loudly nearby.

Four, he was in serious trouble.

He opened his eyes, to find himself in the Ruby Hall of Castle Crimson, surrounded by guards in red livery, before the throne of Bad King Agnemophus. The Bad King was waxing wroth, his normally florid complexion a fiery cherry-red. He was shouting at a princess in a pink gown who clung pitiably to one of the Bad King's tree-trunk legs. As his vision cleared, Nick realized that the girl was Joy, and that Joy was Princess Joyeux, daughter to Agnemophus.

"Father, I love him!"

"Daughter, you are making me very angry!" shouted the Bad King. He must have noticed that Nick was rousing, for he turned the force of his powerful voice upon the poor ropemaker. "And you, peasant, how dare you embrace a princess of the blood royal?" the Bad King bellowed.

Nick raised his throbbing head, and despite his fear, looked levelly into Bad King Agnemophus' eyes and said, "I embraced a girl I fell in love with. I did not know she was a princess, for it was the Crimson Festival."

Princess Joy spoke up then. "And I embraced a boy I fell in love with. I did not know he was a peasant, for it was the Crimson Festival. And I don't care if he's common!"

The Bad King's eyes spun like little tops as he gritted his teeth. "Is that so?"

"Yes, Father," said Joyeux. "I want to marry him."

"Then it matters not if I disinherit you if you persist in this foolishness, stripping you of your rank and titles. Casting you out of the castle. Sending you away from all your servants."

Pridefully, the Princess tossed her head. "I'll accept being made common, for love."

The color of the Bad King's face darkened from cherry to maroon. "I think not." He gestured imperiously to his soldiers. "Guards! Take the Princess away, and imprison her in durance vile upon the Invisible Island until she regains her senses! The very idea!"

The Princess screamed and kicked and pleaded as the guards dragged her away. Nick tried to reach her, standing up on wobbly legs, but one of the Bad King's guards kicked his feet out from under him. Nick fell and smashed his head against the floor. All he was able to do was to cry from his deepest soul, "My heart belongs to you, Joy!"

He felt sausage-sized fingers twining through his hair, then a strong pull as the Bad King yanked Nick up, face-to-face. Nick saw an evil glint in Agnemophus' beady little eyes.

"Since you like to dress up like a sailor so much, commoner, I'm sentencing you to the sea. You will live out the rest of your pitiful life, at hard labor." Bad King Agnemophus laughed and waved to his guards. "Take him away!"

Nick struggled against the guardsmen who were dragging him

out of the Ruby Hall, and was again knocked out.

*   *   *

The prison ship *Zoltaran* was under the command of a cruel captain named Wizzyfig. *Zoltaran* made the treacherous run to the Oversea kingdom of Caferustland, six weeks out and six weeks back, braving storms and sea monsters and pirates galore. For Caferustland was the only reliable source of dragon venom, which Rosso wizards utilized to make firepowder for the cannons of the Rosson army and navy. Dragon venom, thickened and hardened by Caferustlander arts into blue-black ingots, which scalds any bare skin that brushes against it, bursts into flame if sweet water touches it, and gives off noxious fumes if doused with alcohol. No Rosson sailor with half his wits about him would ship with such a cargo, so it was left to the prisoners who crewed the *Zoltaran* to transport the deadly bricks.

Three months went by with Nick a prisoner of the sea. He holystoned the decks, worked the winches, repaired the ropes, ran out the sails, pumped the bilges, loaded the hazardous dragon venom, hoisted the anchor, and pulled the oars when the wind becalmed the ship. He grew stronger, leaner, meaner. The good-nature within him hardened and thickened, much like the vitriolic ingots of dragon venom, focusing his being, refining it.

He grew close to two of his fellow prisoners: Salt McTaffy and Coop Carver.

Salt McTaffy was a gigantic Living Confection, both stretchy and strong. Salt had been sent to the *Zoltaran* because he had fought off some of Agnemophus' guards who were stealing candy from the shop of his maker and master, Aknow Candysmith. He was quiet and easy-going until pushed too far, then Salt would snap into sudden violence... and if it were against the servants of the Bad King, so much the better.

Coop Carver was a magic-man carpenter who whispered to the wood and made it dance to his will. He had been unrightfully imprisoned because Bad King Agnemophus had slammed his royal finger in a cabinet that Coop had made for him. The injustice of his punishment had made Coop a little crazy, which is probably why he went along with the mad plan Nick came up with to win their freedom.

When next the *Zoltaran* put into Caferustland and the prisoners were loading the wicker baskets full of dragon venom ingots, Coop distracted the guards with a wooden songbird he'd made. As the carved figurine whistled and trilled, the guards laughed and clapped, ignoring Nick as he reached under the nearest basket and grabbed a brick that burned and seared his hand. Bravely, he did not cry out, but wrapped the ingot in a piece of sailcloth, then handed it to Salt. Salt calmly jammed the parcel into his chest, and allowed his squishy flesh to flow back over the cloth-wrapped package. By the time the songbird stopped warbling, no one could tell that anything had happened.

It was only after the ship had finished loading and the prisoners were sent below without dinner (as was common, since Wizzyfig was indeed cruel) that Nick showed his friends his useless hand, with its flesh scorched away to the bone, with ashy streaks stretching up the rest of his arm. There was nothing for it but to take the entire arm off, before the dragon venom killed Nick.

In the dead of night, with the help of the ship's doctor (another prisoner), they cut off Nick's poisoned arm. . . and replaced it with a magical wooden one that Coop had carved for him out of a rowboat oar. The wooden arm was cunningly jointed, and quite handsome, actually. And because Nick had been tanned deeply by the sunlight of the Southern Sea, it took a second glance to realize that his new arm was actually artificial. Nick was back at work the next morning, and the guards never noticed anything different about the young prisoner.

Three weeks into the voyage, in the middle of the journey, the next phase of the plan was enacted. Salt extruded the parcel from his chest, and unwrapped the ingot of dragon venom. Coop produced a small keg he'd stolen from the ship's stores, where the three of them had been pouring half their grog ration for the last week. Nick pulled a length of shroudline from his pocket, and worked up a cunning cat's cradle that held the dangerous ingot safely above the grog inside the keg. Then Coop replaced the keg's lid, and Nick attached a short piece of twine that, when yanked, would release the ropes that held the ingot suspended, dropping it into the grog.

And then they waited for the Captain to call for more drink.

As this was the middle of the run, and the guards were getting restive, the call did not take long in coming. Salt carried the keg aft to Wizzyfig's salon, the loop of twine concealed in one massive fist. Meanwhile, Coop produced keys he'd carved from scraps, and he and Nick unlocked the chains that held all of their fellow prisoners captive. They crept forward, towards the arms locker.

Salt entered the Captain's cabin, and set the keg of grog down on the table, where the guards were fairly slavering for more drink. With a rubbery smile at Wizzyfig, he yanked the loop of twine, and the brick of frozen dragon venom fell into the mix of rum and water. Foul smoke and green flames exploded from the keg, making the guards' eyes water and making the Captain scream like a frightened baby. In the confusion, they all went for their swords and pistols, just as Nick, Coop, and the rest of the now freed and armed prisoners burst into the cabin!

The prisoners all fell upon their former captors. Salt's arms stretched and wrapped around the sailors, smashing them together. Coop swung a carpenter's mallet, braining the guards left and right. And Nick, his wooden arm grasping a cutlass, dueled blade to blade with cruel Captain Wizzyfig.

Cruelty does not imply skill, nor courage (quite the opposite), so remarkably soon, our doughty heroes overcame the villainous Wizzyfig and his men.

Soon, the prisoners had won the battle. They disarmed Wizzyfig and the guards, and set them adrift in a longboat. Wizzyfig and his men cursed them as they floated off across the waves, never to be heard from again.

The prisoners claimed the ship *Zoltaran* as their own, deciding to become pirates, preying specifically on ships owing loyalty to Bad King Agnemophus of Rosso. They elected Nick their captain unanimously. Nick made Salt his first mate, and rechristened the ship the *Seeker* – for while he wished as much as his fellows to harm the Bad King, he wished more to discover the location of the Invisible Island, and rescue the prisoner there he loved: Princess Joyeux.

*   *   *

Over the next few months, Captain Knott and the *Seeker* proved a great thorn in Bad King Agnemophus' side. Their depredations hobbled the Rosson navy, captured valuable cargoes, and blocked treasure from flowing into the Bad King's coffers. The Bad King was hard pressed to deal with these reverses, and even considered asking the Zorcerer Himself (Herself? Itself?) for the aid of the Imperial Navy, but decided against it, because once the Zorcerer's attention was drawn to Rosso, *who knows* what secrets His (Hers? Its?) zorcery could uncover that Agnemophus would prefer remained hidden?

So instead, Agnemophus spent even more money outfitting his ships with sailors and cannon. He wooed other pirates to become privateers with promises of gold and pardons for their crimes against him. He consulted with evil sea hags and struck deals with monsters under the waves.

No matter what, Captain Knott and the pirates of the *Seeker* prevailed against the Bad King's forces. They always won in battle, escaped in the nick of time, or avoided the deadly trap. But they were often hard-pressed and suffered losses, no one more than their Captain.

Nick lost his left arm fighting another Pirate Captain, who'd turned privateer for the Bad King: a dangerous duelist known as Swords O'Shanty. He lost his left leg to the Ochre Octopus that haunted the Ripclaw Reef, and his right leg to the spells of the Sand Witch on the Isle of Oyam. His head was even taken off by a cannonball during a sea-battle against the Bad King's flagship, the *Sanguine*.

Luckily, his friend Coop Carver was there to restore each missing piece with a magical wooden replacement. These timber prosthetics were beautiful, functional, and sturdy: hard as steel, light as a feather, smooth as glass, and wonderfully carved, etched, and varnished against the sea air.

All the while, Captain Nick sought information on the location of the Invisible Island. In a noisy tavern in Avalon, he discovered the sea in which it lay: the Sea of Tears. In the middle of a hurricane, he wrestled Typhoon Tom, the Wind Wizard, to determine the distance to said Island. In the long-buried treasure chest of the Pirate Parrot that he dug up on the Island of Bones, he found out the proper bearing.

However, the final hurdle between him and getting to the Invisible Island was one man and one man alone: Captain Jack Dogg, the most deadly pirate of all, now flying Rosso's colors over his ship, the *Maelstrom*.

Captain Knott met Captain Dogg at the World's Edge, where the storms rage forever. Their ships and crews locked in combat among the crashing waves and the rolling thunder. Many on both sides died in bloody, glorious battle.

Nick's men were slowly winning, bringing him ever-closer to reaching the Invisible Island and rescuing his lady love until disaster struck. Captain Dogg revealed his terrible secret: he was not a man at all, but Shaykosch, the Gray Wolf, Death On Four Legs!

His lupine nature displayed for all to see, he killed six of *Seeker's* pirates in one blow. He tore Salt McTaffy apart, throwing half to starboard and half to port. He shattered the deck beneath Coop Carver, sending him plummeting into the lowest hold. And he went blade to blade with Nick.

The fight raged over deck, up shrouds, across masts and booms, and down ratlines and sails. Sparks flashed like the lighting in the sky and clashes rang like thunder when their cutlasses met. Smoke and steam rose from them as they fought like demons.

Eventually, they were face to face, weaving nets of steel around each other, in a rowboat, drifting away from the wreckage of the *Seeker* and the *Maelstrom*, towards the World's Edge itself. Nick kept silent, his wooden teeth clenched tight, while Shaykosch laughed as if all the death and destruction were simply a lark to him.

But the monster stopped laughing when Nick clipped off his left ear. With a howl that shook the sky, he summoned the wolves of the seas to his aid: an entire shiver of Lightning Sharks. Under his command, they snapped and leapt at Nick, teeth striking sparks and skins sizzling like skillets. "Under my control, they will rip your gizzard out, Captain Knott. And when the blood frenzy strikes them, they'll chew even your wooden bits to splinters, and no one – not even me! – can stop them!"

His wooden face impassive, Nick then knew exactly what must be done. He turned his cutlass against himself, against the last bits of flesh, blood, and bone he possessed: his human torso. Gutting himself like a fish, he spilled his innards into the churning sea, giving the Lightning Sharks their first taste of blood. However, his wooden left hand nimbly flashed out and caught his still-beating heart before it could tumble into the reddening ocean.

Nick's blood in the water made the beasts go crazy. Lightning arced between them, crackling and hissing even above the roar of the storm. They thrashed like lunatics, and tried to flop into the rowboat.

Shaykosch stood dumfounded: first by Nick's opening himself up like a trout, second by his sudden and irreparable loss of command over the Lightning Sharks, and third by Nick squirting him with the blood from his own human heart, which he held grimly in one hand. The Gray Wolf was so confused, that when the heavy timber of Nick's right leg kicked him in the muzzle, he fell right into the sea, and the middle of the frenzied shiver of sharks.

The Lightning Sharks tore Shaykosch to pieces, and the monster was lost to the world for a span of years.

For his part, Nick made his way slowly back to the *Seeker*, holding his chest closed with one hand – otherwise, it'd flap like a greatcoat in the wind – and gripping his heart tightly with the other. Back on the ship, Coop made him a new torso out of an old sea chest, which even had a set of drawers within. Nick placed his heart in the top left drawer, atop a silken handkerchief.

(Meanwhile, the two halves of Salt McTaffy had been gathered up and placed together in a cauldron in the ship's galley. While the parts melted and flowed together into one whole, Salt did not awake until much later, when Nick took his comatose friend to see his maker: Aknow Candysmith… but that is another tale.)

After the *Maelstrom* had been pillaged and the *Seeker* repaired, Captain Knott set sail for the Invisible Island and his Princess.

*　　*　　*

The *Seeker* barreled into the harbor of the Invisible Island in the dark of night, under cover of fog. They landed quickly, and the pirates swarmed over the sides of the ship onto the dock, led by their wooden captain. They overpowered the wharf guards easily, and made for the Lonely Tower where the Princess was held in durance vile.

The tower guards, surprised out of their sleep on this normally uneventful duty, fell like wheat before the reapers at harvest time. Nick's wooden legs clunked as he ran up the long stair to the room at the top of the tower. With three powerful blows from his timber arms, the barred door blocking him from his objective fell. He stood, framed in the doorway, and called into the darkness for his love.

"Colonel, your Admiral has come to rescue you."

"Oh Nick, my love!" cried the Princess as she ran to her shadowed savior. The two of them embraced briefly, before Princess Joyeux pulled away in confusion. "What's wrong with your chest? With your arms?" – and when Nick turned and the light from the hallway struck him in full – "Oh, Nick, what has happened to your handsome face?"

Nick smiled, his wooden lips creaking slightly. "Finding and freeing you has been a long and torturous quest, my Princess. I have suffered much, but all for the sake of love. All for the sake of you."

Joyeux pushed him away. "I never asked for this," she said petulantly. "You're just a thing of timber, planks, and driftwood now. How can a Princess love a tinkertoy?"

Nick's faced fell and his wooden eyes widened. "But I am the same, inside. I am still the man you love."

"I loved a man, a man of flesh and blood. You're nothing but a Wooden Pirate now."

Stunned like Shaykosch at the World's Edge, Nick felt something inside of himself change. His heart stopped beating within his wooden chest, the thumping vibration of it ceasing, forever. His eyes narrowed. His wooden fingers flexed, as if to go for the hilt of his trusty cutlass, but instead opened up the front of his torso on its brass hinges.

"I said once that this belongs to you." Reaching inside, he opened the top left drawer, withdrew his stilled heart, and dropped it at Princess Joyeux's feet right there on the floor of her cell. "Do with it what you will." Then he spun on his heel and walked away, down the tower stairs, out to the dock, and boarded the *Seeker*.

After his crew had finished sacking the Rosson garrison, plundering it of supplies and treasure, the Wooden Pirate ordered them to hoist anchor and set sail. They sailed into the rising sun, leaving the ungrateful Princess crying behind on the shore of the Invisible Island, surrounded by the wreckage.

The Wooden Pirate plagued Bad King Agnemophus for many years after leaving his heart at the feet of Princess Joyeux. . . but that's another tale.

THE END

Galen and the Golden-Coat Hare

By Jon F. Zeigler

Once upon a time, in the faraway land of Azul, there lived a poor huntsman named Galen . . .

Galen dwelt with his wife Katherine on the margin of the mysterious Fogwood. There he hunted for game large and small, while his wife did fine needlework and kept geese and chickens. They sold what they did not need in the nearest village, and bought what they did need. Life was not easy for them, but Galen rarely complained.

One day, Galen was in the bluewood, bow at the ready, checking his snare traps. As he approached the shadowy place where he had laid out his third snare, he heard a thrashing noise in the brush, as of a small creature desperately struggling for freedom.

Galen slung his bow and moved closer. He moved a little brush aside and looked to see what he had caught.

For a long moment, surprise held him still.

A hare. Lanky body, powerful hind legs, long ears, wide eyes, it all said *hare*. The only thing to say otherwise was the creature's *color*: shimmering, shining gold. Not dull brown, not off-white, not buttery yellow, not any of the usual hare-colors, but *gold* like a coin Galen had once seen from afar off in a nobleman's hand. It looked like wealth and ease and a hundred acres of land in that one creature's pelt.

It can't really be gold, he asked himself. *Can it?*

Galen pushed the brush aside further and stepped toward the snare.

At once, the hare stopped thrashing about and stared at him. Then it **spoke**.

"Oh kind sir, please wait!"

Galen stopped. *Well. This changes things.*

"Please stay your hand!" said the hare. "Set me free and I will reward you greatly!"

The hare did not *look* like a Talking Animal. It had a frame ill-suited for walking on two feet. It wore no clothing and carried no tools. In all ways other than that tempting pelt, it appeared a perfectly ordinary beast. Quite suitable for the pot.

"Oh mighty huntsman, I have a doe and kits to think of. They will starve without my watchful care. Please spare me!"

On the other hand, the hare certainly *sounded* like a Talking Animal. Indeed, it sounded remarkably like a dishonest tinker who had wandered through the village a few months before. Galen grunted and made up his mind. He stepped forward once more, drawing his knife and bending over the snare.

"Oh no oh dear oh please *I will grant you three wishes if you spare my life* . . ."

Galen put a strong hand over the hare, which struggled mightily. "Hold still, you foolish creature!"

Something in the timbre of the man's voice got through the hare's fright. Heart racing, breath panting, it froze in place.

Galen slipped the knife under the snare and cut through the cord. He then lifted his hand, releasing his prey.

Quick as lightning, the hare was off into the underbrush. Galen heard leaves rustle for just a moment, and then all fell silent.

He sighed as he collected the pieces of the cut snare. "Two hours' work gone for nothing," he muttered to himself.

"Not for nothing, kind sir!" came a voice from the underbrush. "I promised you three wishes, and three wishes you shall have."

"No need," said Galen shortly. "You're free to go."

There was a moment of profound silence.

"*What?*" asked the hare.

"I don't need any wishes granted. I didn't set you free for them. I make it a rule never to kill Talking Animals, for their meat or for their pelt or for any reason at all. It's a good rule. Never steered me wrong yet. Off you go."

"But . . ."

"Off you go, I said. Shoo."

Silence from the underbrush.

Galen placed the pieces of his snare in his pack, carefully cleaned and sheathed his knife, and then turned to depart.

The golden-coat hare ventured a few inches back out into the open, just enough to show wiggling nose and bright eyes. "Are you *certain* I cannot interest you in any wishes?"

"Quite certain."

"Not for wealth? Not for power?"

"Not for anything in the Empire of Zo."

"But . . ."

"I have work to do. Goodbye."

With that Galen left the clearing, the golden-coat hare sitting bemused and confused in his wake.

*   *   *

Naturally, that did not end the story.

By late afternoon Galen returned home, fresh herbs in his pack and a brace of thoroughly nonverbal rabbits hanging from his belt. "I am home, wife, and I have dinner."

Katherine emerged from their cottage, brushing flour from her hands. "Good. I was just making apple dumplings. Bring some water in from the well, if you would."

"At once, after I have skinned and cleaned these coneys."

She nodded with a smile and went back inside, leaving the door open.

"A strange thing happened today," said Galen, as he drew his knife and began to skin the rabbits.

"What was it?"

"I caught a hare in one of my snares. Very strange in appearance, it was. Pelt like gold."

"That is strange. Do you say it *was* gold?"

"I doubt it. Beast with true gold for its fur would have a difficult time living. Would weight it down, make it hard to scamper. Still, 'twas a remarkable sight to be sure."

"Do you not have the beast?"

"No." Galen finished skinning the rabbits, and began to clean and cut up the carcasses. "It spoke to me, and you know my rule about such things. I let it go."

"Too bad. I would like to have seen it."

"Aye. It offered me three wishes . . ."

Clang: the sound of a ladle falling into an iron pot. At once, Katherine stood in the doorway once more, staring down at her husband where he sat working. "Three wishes? How many have you already used?"

"None, wife, nor will I use any. It was no true bargain. I did not release the beast for the sake of any gain."

"Galen!" She stepped around to confront him, hands on her hips, silver-grey eyes flashing in anger. "Such an opportunity, and you threw it away?"

He paused to give her a wary stare. "What opportunity? No good comes from wishing. Hard work and fair dealing are the only way for any honest man to gain."

Katherine rolled her eyes. "Galen, sometimes I despair of you. We could have so much more than this cottage on the forest's edge. We could have land, and coin enough for anything we might need." She sighed, looking away from him in sadness. "We could have children."

"We could also have sausages on the ends of our noses." He glanced up at her. His hands were bloody, so he kept them at his side, but all the love of his heart lived in his eyes. "Katherine, I know our life is not easy, but at least we can rely upon it. We know this cottage will not fall on us while we sleep, we know the fireplace will draw and the roof will not leak, because we built all of it with our own hands. Wishes are tricky things, and no one ever came out the better for them. And children will come if the Lion sees fit to bless us."

"I suppose you're right," she said at last with a sigh. "You usually are."

"I am sorry." He set his work aside, walked down to the well and washed his hands in the trough, then began to work the crank to draw more water. "Perhaps the world would be a merrier place if it were not so. I wish . . ."

He stopped, because at once the whole world went silent, and seemed to be leaning over him, listening intently.

"Galen?"

"Never mind. I can see that I will have to discipline my words."

* * *

Men considered Galen lucky. He disagreed, not believing in luck. After his encounter with the golden-coat hare, he found even less reason to believe in *good* luck.

No matter how much care and skill he applied when moving through the bluewood, dry twigs and hidden puddles seemed to seek out his feet. He set out snares and found them broken and empty the next day. He drew and aimed at a magnificent stag, only to have his best bowstring break at the point of highest tension. A torrential rain positioned itself over the Fogwood and remained there, driving all creatures into shelter, for days on end.

Each day, he saw the hare at least once – sitting on a distant hill or vanishing into the undergrowth on a dark forest path. Watching him. Waiting.

Galen stubbornly continued to hunt, or at least make the attempt. He had a duty.

Of course, he and his wife still had the geese and chickens. They would not starve for a while, so long as the fowl continued to thrive.

Then, some creature got into the yard in the night, slaying the rooster and half of the hens, all without making a sound. Not even the geese raised any alarm. Galen and Katherine only learned of the slaughter the next morning, when the rooster failed to crow. Whatever beast it was, it carried none of its victims off to be eaten. Katherine accounted for all of them in the morning, dead in a welter of their own blood.

It was simple murder.

The remaining hens, terrified, ceased to lay.

Late that afternoon, the hare sat on a nearby hill and watched, the golden sunlight shining on its coat. As Galen returned from another futile day in the Fogwood, he saw the creature and cursed it under his breath.

You are my enemy. You are the cause of all this misfortune.

Fast as lightning, his bow leapt to his hand, an arrow on the string, and he sighted on the hare.

It did not flee. Slow as an insult, it simply rose on its hind legs as if to offer a better target.

Galen stood still for a long moment, his bow at full extension, a single drop of sweat sliding down his face. Then he eased back, letting his weapon drop.

"*Pah*," he spat. "What use?"

The hare seemed to nod to itself. Then it came loping down the hill, stopping just out of range of a sudden vengeful lunge.

"So. Are you ready for your wishes now?"

Galen grimaced. "After what you have done to me over the past days, you think I am *more* likely to accept a boon from you?"

"I?" The hare used its front paws to brush out its whiskers. "I have done nothing. A word of counsel here and there, a favor or two called in, nothing more."

"I spared your life," said Galen. "I freed you. I asked nothing in return. This is how you repay me?"

"I only hope to do you a good turn, in a manner that befits my nature. Nothing you have suffered is beyond repair by way of a well-considered wish." Its ears twitched and a note of unmistakable *threat* crept into its voice. "*So far*, at any rate."

At once, Galen's knife was in his hand. "Hear me well, creature. Cease this persecution and be away from me and mine. If I see you again, I will learn just how much that golden pelt will fetch in the marketplace."

"No need for that, good sir. This can all be over in a trice. Three wishes."

Then the hare leaped aside in the blink of an eye, Galen's knife quivering in the soil where it had stood a moment before.

"Ah, well," said the golden creature, running at full tilt for the cover of the nearby trees. "You'll change your mind soon enough."

Galen stood for a long moment, trembling with rage. Then he shook his head violently to regain control, and reclaimed his knife.

"The sky will fall first," he muttered.

*   *   *

Galen saw nothing of the hare for the next few days. Yet, the flood of misfortune did not end. Indeed, it *spread*. It began to afflict

97

other hunters who worked the marge of the Fogwood, and then it crept into the village itself.

Farmyard beasts were savaged or driven away. Milk soured in the churn. Nests of stinging insects took up residence in roofs and storage sheds. Flocks of birds began to ignore scarecrows, sweeping down to eat grain in the fields.

Somehow, everyone knew that Galen bore the blame. No one could say where the rumors had begun, but soon everyone was repeating them. He had brought down a curse. He practiced witchcraft against his neighbors. He consorted with the Wolf.

That last struck him to his core.

For the first time, Galen began to feel real fear.

He had few places to turn for advice. Aside from Katherine, he didn't feel enough trust for almost anyone. Given the state of misrule in the kingdom, he had no lord upon whom he could safely rely. Certainly, Count Alphonse would be of no help.

Finally, he decided to visit Friar Benedictus. The friar was a kindly beast, a rotund Talking Hedgehog who wore a clerical habit over his spines and balanced a pair of absurdly tiny spectacles on his snout. He had no magic that anyone could see, but he had the benefit of a fine education, a healer's touch, unshakeable faith in the Lion, and a caring heart. He took no sides in anyone's dispute, and his advice usually proved to be good. Everyone trusted him.

Benedictus did not spend all his time in the village, to be sure. Like any mendicant, he moved about the region, performing whatever service he could to humans, Talking Animals, and even wild beasts. Most people in need knew where to find him. It was Thunder's Day, so the friar could most likely be found in a forest clearing a few miles from the village, tending to the creatures that lived close by. Thorns from rabbits' feet, splinters from beavers' teeth, that sort of thing.

Galen set out just after dawn, his bow and knife at hand. Just in case a certain golden-coat hare chose to make an appearance.

For once, his luck seemed sound. He saw no signs of his enemy or any other uncanny creature. He found the friar hard at work in the expected place, gathering herbs and willow-bark.

The friar looked up sharply as Galen arrived, peered through his spectacles, then bobbed in friendly greeting. "Galen. A pleasure to see you."

"Likewise, Brother." Galen sat down on a boulder and watched as the friar finished his task. "I wondered if I might have a word."

"Of course." Benedictus stood upright, stretching his back with a grunt of pleasure. "Ah, I find I'm not as able to bend over for long as when I was young."

Galen only nodded, looking dour.

"There's quite a shadow on your face, my friend." The friar leaned against a broad tree and produced a small canteen from inside his habit, handing it to Galen. "Apple cider. Very good. Also, very strong."

Galen took a long swig from the canteen, his face softening slightly. "I see what you mean."

"Robert the arborist's son sets aside some from each pressing for me. " A smile, the canteen vanishing back into the habit. "What troubles you, Galen?"

Galen told his story, from the moment he first saw the golden-coat hare. Benedictus listened in silence, his whiskers setting into a concerned frown as the hunter continued to speak.

"I see the problem," said Benedictus at the last.

"What would you advise me to do?"

"I'm not sure. I fear you have placed yourself in the hands of a capricious power." Benedictus stroked his whiskers with one paw. "I believe I recognize this creature, from your description. It is clearly not a simple Talking Animal. It is an enchanted thing, one of the Faerie."

"Katherine and I do what we can to appease such. We put cream and scraps of bread out for the Little People."

"Most of the Little People do not offer to grant wishes. For all that this thing appears to be a helpless beast, it must have great power for its kind. It must be one of the Fair Folk."

Galen shook his head. "How can I contend with such a thing?"

"Perhaps contending with it is the wrong course," said the friar with a sharp glance. "Galen, my friend, if you have a fault, it is that you are *too* self-reliant. In every man's life, there comes a time when he must place his faith in another."

"It goes against my grain," the hunter grumbled.

"No doubt." The friar finished picking his herbs, and began to delicately pack them up. "Two pieces of advice, then, if you are willing to hear them."

Galen nodded in agreement.

"First: the creatures of Faerie are very much bound by their own laws. That may be why this golden-coat hare bedevils you about its three wishes."

"I don't follow you, Brother."

"You saw the creature and seemed about to kill it. It promised you three wishes if you set it free. *You set it free.* By its own word, it *must* now grant you those wishes. It owes you a debt; the longer the books remain open, the more it will suffer. The Fair Ones often seem capricious, but once they give their word, they are tied to it with bands of iron. For one of us, to break a promise is only a sin that may be forgiven. For them, it is a matter of life and death."

"But that is absurd!" Galen shouted. "I freed it for my own reasons. I placed it under no obligation."

"I suspect the hare does not see it that way. By its way of thinking, if you are unwilling to resolve its problem, it has the right to torment you until you do. It may even enjoy the process. Such creatures do not love men."

"That fits," said Galen, nodding slowly. "There is a . . . a *smugness* about the beast. As if it knows that it holds power over me, and I must ere long give in."

"Yes. Now for my second piece of advice. Remember that the Faerie have their own society. This hare must have superiors, lords of its own kind to whom it owes fealty. Perhaps you may appeal to them."

"That sounds even more dangerous than dealing with the one creature."

"Perhaps."

The hunter sat on his rock and thought hard, supporting his chin on one fist. "All right," he said at last.

"Do you see a way forward?"

"Not yet. Or perhaps I see the beginnings of a way."

"Good," said the friar. "Send to let me know how this all turns out. And if I can be of any further help, call on me at once. Such creatures cannot be permitted to get the better of honest people."

*   *   *

Galen heard the first sign of trouble some distance off: Katherine's voice, raised in a shout. He hurried, but not at break-neck speed. He could hear anger in his wife's voice, but no fear or pain.

At the very edge of the forest, he crouched for a moment in shadow to see what lay ahead.

Katherine, standing in the foreyard, fists on her hips, her stance shouting of stubborn pride and resistance. She confronted three men in blue livery. Count Alphonse's men.

Bow in hand, arrow at the string but pointing down for the moment, Galen strode out into the sunlight. "What passes here?" he shouted.

One of the blue-clad men stepped forward, his hand open in token of peace. "I am Simon de Clare, in the service of the Count of Cobaltia. We are here to investigate rumors of trouble."

"There is no trouble here," said Galen, halting within the edge of the ideal range for a quick shot. "I thank you for your concern, but you are wasting your time."

"It is our time to waste." De Clare glanced around the yard, his eyes missing nothing. "You are Galen Chasseur?"

"I am, as anyone in the village could tell you."

"You are accused of witchcraft and consorting with evil spirits. What say you?"

"Pfah!" Galen scowled. "Who accuses me? I have a right to face him."

"Only if the accusation is formal. Thus far, it is not. We hope to resolve the situation without requiring such measures."

"Then I say the accusation is groundless. I know there is a curse at work, but it is none of my doing. We have suffered from it as much as any. I have no grudge against any of my neighbors, nor should they have any cause for a quarrel with me."

"I see." De Clare nodded in satisfaction and turned back to Galen. "Well, I am inclined to take the word of such an honest fellow."

Galen nodded in thankful suspicion.

"Of course . . . should it be proven that you are *not* an honest fellow, I would have to reconsider. Which brings me to another matter of concern. I took the time to examine the village rolls before coming here. To my surprise, I found that you have no right to live here, or to hunt in the Fogwood."

"What? I have land-right and forest-right, clear as day in the village rolls."

"Ah, but you have those rights by way of your father, who had them from the last King. Have you sworn an oath of fealty for the renewal of those rights?"

"There's no one to swear fealty *to*, unless the Heir should return."

De Clare spread his hands in helplessness. "You see my problem. By law, you are a poacher and a thief, not an honest man at all. So how may I take your word that you are not the cause of the curse afflicting this village?"

"That's not what the law says, and you know it."

"Perhaps. I suppose we could take this to the village court. Where the case would be tried by your peers. Most of whom are already half-convinced that you are a sorcerer. Or . . ." De Clare paused as if in thought.

"Spit it out, man," said Galen in disgust.

"My master could doubtless resolve all of this, if you were willing to swear fealty to *him*. Become his man, support his claim to the throne, convince your neighbors to do the same. He will advise the Mayor and the village to let the matter rest. You could make your fortune in his service."

"I see." Galen sighed. "All this trouble goes away, and the Count makes me a rich man. All I have to do is become a lying lickspittle like yourself."

De Clare smiled gently. "You do seem to have grasped the situation."

"Never."

"Well. That *is* too bad, but I shouldn't take your first answer. Think about the matter while I report back to my master and hear his answer. You have perhaps three days to consider."

"Three days or three years, my answer will be the same."

All at once, de Clare's manner of polished courtesy vanished. "For your own sake, it had better not be. When I return, I will have more than two men with me."

Then he turned on his heel, the other two following, and strode away.

Galen stood, his bow still in his hand pointing at nothing, until he felt a presence at his side.

"Husband," Katherine said, "I am proud of you."

He released the breath he had been holding. "You should not be. I got us into this."

"No. You are not the one in the wrong." She hesitated. "Still . . . I admit to being afraid."

"So am I, love."

"What are we going to do?"

He reached out and put an arm around her shoulders. "The only thing we can do. Live each day and look for a way out."

"Galen . . ." She sighed. "You are the most unimaginative man I have ever known. Bless you."

He snorted. "Be that as it may, I still have work to do."

"Come inside in an hour. I will have fresh bread and broth for you."

Galen went down to the well, and then to check the fowl-yard. No more of the birds had been slain in the night.

From the cottage, a harsh *crack*. Then Katherine's voice, this time full of pain.

When Galen looked back, he saw the roof of his cottage falling in.

He ran.

*　　*　　*

The roof-tree of the cottage had suddenly failed, crashing down to the floor. Galen was able to drag Katherine out to safety. Under his breath, he thanked the Lion she had taken nothing worse than some bruises and a broken arm.

It was almost sunset before Katherine finally fell asleep. Friar Benedictus had done what he could, setting the bone and giving her poultices and a sleeping draught. Yet, even in her sleep, she whimpered with the pain. When the friar emerged from the cottage's front door, he found Galen sitting on a stool, turning a piece of wood over and over in his hands.

"Dry rot," said the hunter. "See here, Brother? Just at one end of the roof-tree. So corrupt that it couldn't hold the weight of the roof in place any longer."

"A terrible accident," said Benedictus.

"No accident," Galen said flatly. "I built this cottage with my own hands. The wood was sound. This much rot, and the frame would not have held the roof in place for an instant."

"What are you saying?"

"The Fair Folk cannot abide the touch of cold iron, nor can their magic bite upon it. They could not have attacked the iron of the nails that held the frame together. But the *wood* of the frame itself, *that* they could corrupt. To cause it to rot, all in an instant, just when my Katherine was standing there in the way."

Benedictus nodded slowly.

Galen sighed and stood. "Brother, I'm ready to end this now. Will you stand with me?"

"Gladly, my friend."

Galen cast the scrap of wood aside. He stepped out into the fading light and looked around, as if seeking his enemy. "All right, you damnable creature! Come out and face me. I'm ready to make my first wish."

The golden-coat hare emerged from behind Galen's well, where it must have been waiting for just such a pronouncement. It almost wriggled with glee as it hopped across the yard.

"About time," it said. "You might have avoided so much trouble had you seen reason sooner."

Galen only spat, missing the hare by inches.

"Rude. So what will your first wish be? Something simple: healing for your wife, game for your bag, forgiveness from your friends? Or will it be more of the usual human greed: gold, land, victory in battle, power over others? So many possibilities. Come now, let's hear it."

"You will." Galen's fists balled at his sides as he stared at the hare. "*I wish for justice.*"

The hare ceased to move. Its nose, its whiskers, its ears became absolutely still. Its eyes stopped gleaming with delight and grew dull. It hunched low on its legs, as if hoping to evade notice.

Friar Benedictus breathed a heavy sigh of relief. "Oh, *well done*, Galen."

Far off in the distance, they heard a sound of trumpets.

Soon, a procession appeared at the brow of the hill behind Galen's land, moving with speed and grace toward where the hunter and the hare waited. Handsome men in bright-colored tunics and hose, beautiful women in sheer white gowns, all of them seemed to glow from within despite the failing light of the sun. Galen and Friar Benedictus stood spell-bound, watching that fair company as it approached.

The Fair Folk arrived, their voices like chimes and woodwinds, and stopped a few paces off. Their company parted, revealing their leader.

Dwarfish he was, his head not quite coming up to Galen's heart, but handsome and well-formed as any of his people. His hair was dark as a starless night, his eyes cornflower-blue and shining with merriment. His voice, when he spoke, had the tone of a waldhorn singing alone in the deep forest. "Not long ago as the sunlit lands measure time, I heard rumor of ill-working among my people. I am on my way to Midsummer revels in a faraway land, yet such matters *must* take precedence. *Whom* do I see before me?"

The friar stepped forward and bowed. "Lord Alberich, I am Friar Benedictus. This is Galen, a huntsman, who holds himself wronged by one of your subjects."

The dwarf glanced at Galen for barely a moment, and then his eyes fell on the golden-coat hare. "How now, young Puck? What have you to say to this?"

"I have done this man no wrong," said the hare with indignation. "Indeed, I have offered him three boons, which he has not the wit to use."

Friar Benedictus glanced at Galen and felt his eyes widen in surprise. The hunter positively *swelled* with anger, losing his temper for the first time since anyone could easily recall.

"No wrong?" shouted Galen. "Shall we speak of game scared off, fowl slain, milk soured, grain eaten out of the fields, children stung, elders sickened? Shall we speak of my wife, lying there with a fearsome hurt? Shall we speak of my neighbors turned against me, the Count's men ready to lay hand on me? And you say I have not been *wronged?*"

"Have you done all these things, Puck?"

The hare took up a posture of affronted dignity. "Certainly not."

"They were done at this creature's bidding," said Galen.

Alberich looked stern. "Would any these things have come to pass without your will?"

The hare shifted its weight. "Well . . . no."

"Then why did you convince others to harm this man, his neighbors, and his wife?"

"Because I *owe* him three wishes!" The hare looked away. "Two now. You know what I must suffer, with such a debt unpaid."

"Beware, golden runner in the fields, for I can see to your shivering heart, and I know this to be a lie." Alberich stepped closer, his face like a thundercloud. "I see no signs of suffering in you at all. Indeed, you seem well-fed, well-groomed, and well-satisfied. Explain this."

Galen's eyes narrowed as he watched the hare, a suspicion taking root in his heart.

"I can't, oh great and terrible lord," quavered the hare.

"I can," said Galen.

"Indeed?" said Alberich with surprise. "Please do so."

"The last time I saw this beast, this Puck, I threw my knife at it. I am a knife-man of no common wit. Where I throw, I strike. Yet, this hare dodged aside in the blink of an eye."

"Our Puck is no common beast," said the dwarf.

"Perhaps. But that isn't all. Before the knife, I had my bow at full draw and had sighted down on the creature. I am an archer of no common wit. Where I shoot, I strike. Yet this hare stood stock-still, as if it had nothing at all to fear."

"I *did* have nothing to fear, you fool!" The hare danced from paw to paw in reckless pride.

"Then how is it that you were caught by one of my snares?"

Silence.

"A snare?" asked Alberich in wonder. "Our Puck was caught and held . . . by a *snare?*"

"A common snare, made of wood and leather and not an ounce of cold iron," said Galen. "Yet there it lay, helpless and ready to be slain. Or so it seemed."

Galen did not expect what came next.

Alberich and all his company *laughed.*

Galen had heard much laughter in his day, even if he was not normally inclined to join in. Joyful laughter, laughter at a jest, these things he understood. The laughter of the Fair Folk bore nothing of such honest merriment. It spoke instead of inhuman cruelty and spite. It spoke of death, of children starving alone in the forest, of fresh blood bathing a stone under the full moon.

He shivered. *May the Lion keep all creatures such as these far away from me. Assuming I live through this night.*

He glanced at Benedictus as the laughter died away, seeing the friar's eyes wide with fear. Then he turned back to the Faerie King.

"You see it now. This creature was never in danger of being caught in my snare. It could have freed itself at any time, by withering the snare as it did my roof-tree. When I freed it, I did nothing it could not have done for itself. It owes me no obligation at all. Every hurt it has done to me and to my neighbors has been an unprovoked crime. Even by your folk's lights, I think."

"Indeed," said Alberich. "My people hold no love for yours, Man, for your greed, your cold iron, and your ravaging of the earth. But those who cry for justice may not act unjustly in their turn. I deem that to punish you for a harm that never was – well, it is a crime. Puck!"

The golden-coat hare shivered, and then seemed to *grow*. In the space of two breaths, the hare was gone and a small golden man stood in its place. "I hear, oh terrible King."

"This is my Doom: you shall wander the Fogwood in the form of a hare, robbed of your voice and your cunning, so that you may learn what it is to be toyed with by greater powers. You shall be left with your swiftness, your fear, and nothing else. So shall it be for a year and a day. If you survive so long, well and done."

Puck bowed his head. "So be it."

"You will also hear this Word: never again shall you attempt to force a boon upon any man, neither by force nor by fraud. If you do, be very certain. ***I will feed you to Shaykosch***."

The golden-skinned man trembled in terror. "I understand."

"Then go!"

The last of the sun's light shone on Puck as he returned to his lapine shape. Then, a streak of gold ran through the grass, and he was gone.

"Now, huntsman, justice demands that I make things right." Alberich peered at Galen, his blue eyes shining with an uncanny light. "What boons would you ask of *me* to see that done?"

Friar Benedictus gave Galen a warning glance, but the huntsman only gave a grim smile.

"None, my lord, except that all of us harmed by Puck's malice be made whole."

"A human with wisdom and lacking in greed," observed the dwarf. "The Powers Above stand still in amazement at such a sight. So mote it be."

"Thank you, lord Alberich."

"Thanks? What need have I of your thanks, Man?"

Galen shrugged. "None, I daresay. But isn't courtesy always worthwhile?"

"Perhaps." The dwarf lord smiled.

Alberich turned to his people. "Now then, let us be at our work, so that we may attend our revels on time! Healing to the sick and injured, new beasts brought to those who have lost theirs, wasps tamed and serpents driven aside! Food of the best: meat, cheese, fresh bread and ale, all of a kind good for mortals, for all those who have gone hungry! This cottage rebuilt sounder than before! In every ear, whisper that Galen the huntsman is free of blame, and that the Fair Folk always pay their debts! Be off now, in a twinkling!"

So it was done, and the Fair Folk departed under the first light of the stars. Galen and Katherine invited the friar into their cottage to share of their new bounty.

And did they live happily ever after? Perhaps . . . but that is another story.

THE END

The Horse Prince

by Chad Underkoffler

Once Upon A Time, in the Land of Zo. . .

There was a kingdom called Giallo, to the west of the Jade City, capital of Zo. Breadbasket of the Empire, its vast plains of grass and wheat had had no single ruler for generations, after the royal line of the Giallons died out. Instead, it was a patchwork of fiefdoms – duchies, principalities, counties, marches – ruled by a number of nobles of Human and Talking Animal descent.

One such ruler was Huvaz, the Horse Prince. He led the Long-Stepper Tribe of Fourfoot Talking Horses in their nomadic journeys around Giallo. In these peregrinations, his tribe would war, feast, and trade at turns with the more settled folk and leaders of the kingdom (like the Star-Strider Tribe of Twofoot Talking Horses that lived in the village of Triticum, the forces of the villainous – and hugely fat! – Roly-Poly Prince, the subtle and sleek vulpine guilds of Cuidad Llwynog, and the elegant and deadly Marquis de Carabas). The Long-Steppers, from time before time, have always been spoken of with respect – and not a little fear – and during Huvaz's reign, this was just as so.

Scholars of Zo have long asked: how did Huvaz rise to the leadership of such a puissant and freedom-loving people? He was not the swiftest of the Tribe (though he was speedy). He was not the strongest of the Tribe (though he was brawny). He was not the smartest of the Tribe (though he was canny). How then could he match his fellows in struggles of speed, strength, or wits?

The answer is simple. Though he had not the greatest speed, strength, or intelligence of his fellows, what Huvaz possessed in abundance – more so than any before or since! – was *perseverance*. In contests of endurance of effort, stamina of body, study of mind, or tenacity of soul, he had no equal.

Once, he ran untiring to deliver medicine to cure his love, Princess Shoalla of the Star-Strider Tribe – from the Astronomical Apothecary of Jade City in Zo Proper to Triticum on the edge of the Pancake Plains: over a hundred and thirty-seven leagues in distance. Fifty leagues a day Huvaz ran, and in three days he crossed the span, in a shorter time than even the fastest (but less resilient) braves of his Tribe could assay.

Captured by treachery by the Roly-Poly Prince, he was put to work driving the millwheel of the tyrant's Great Granary. For a week, he was neither fed, nor watered, nor allowed to rest. He was repeatedly beaten with whips. Still, in the one slim second for the opportunity for escape arose, iron-boned Huvaz was ready. He burst his bonds, killed his jailers with thunderous hoof-blows, and freed his fellow captives from their imprisonment.

Huvaz once played chess with the Marquis de Carabas, in order to determine who had the priority of trading rights with the King of Azul. Over three straight days, seventeen games they played ceaselessly, until the Horse Prince came out the victor against his yawning feline rival.

When the fox-guilds of Cuidad Llwynog tried to drive up the cost of their blankets and oats (which they traded to the Long-Steppers for the rare and mystical herbs the Horse Tribe gathered in their travels), Huvaz refused to play their game. His people, though they needed the blankets and oats, were not as desperate as the fox-folk were for their magic spices. His thirteen-month embargo of the vulpine traders eventually brought them to their knees and reason.

And when the tax-collectors of the Zorcerer himself mandated that the Long-Stepper Tribe settle down, tying themselves to the land, to ease the collection of tithes for their master, Huvaz stood firm. "For a thousand moons, we have roamed Giallo," the Horse Prince said. "We will not stop our wanderings for the Zorcerer, be he Man or Beast." For seven years, he and his tribe resisted the cajoling, the threats, the armed forces of the tax-collectors. And through Huvaz's impossible obduracy, the Zorcerer Himself (Herself? Itself?) was eventually brought to an accommodation, out of respect for Huvaz's strength of will. Even today, under the laws of Zo, the Long-Steppers are unrestrained in their roaming, if they but pay their tribute to the Zorcerer once a year at Carabas. The Horse Prince agreed to this arrangement, and it was so then as it is now.

Indeed, it was Huvaz's traveling to Carabas to deliver the Zorcerer's tithe that begins this tale of valor. Taking with him only three of his most stalwart braves, he brought to Carabas the spoils of the year: weaponry taken from the forces of the Roly-Poly Prince's men, those rare and valuable herbs that only grew in the hinterlands of the Empire, new songs and mysteries for analysis and contemplation. All were acceptable tribute for the Zorcerer.

When Huvaz and his braves returned to the encampment of the Long-Steppers, the Prince discovered a thing of horror: Shaykosch, the Gray Wind, the Great Enemy, had appeared in his absence.

Shaykosch! The Deathless Wolf. The Great Adversary of Zo from time immemorial. Shifter of shape, master of dark magics, blooded warrior of great skill; the Gray Wind, proverbial in his swiftness, strength, and cunning. Defeated – even killed! – again and again by the greatest heroes of the Empire, the Wolf had always returned. Thief, murderer, traitor – all begin to describe Shaykosch, but do not even come close to the depths of his villainy!

In Huvaz's absence, the evil Wolf had challenged the doughtiest warrior of the tribe. With laughing ease, he killed the one that stood against him: Duuron the Strong. Then the Wolf had stolen the wealth of the tribe (blankets, oats, secrets, joy) and moved on.

Now, Huvaz had never liked Duuron. Since they were foals, the two of them had been in competition. They had fought over status within the tribe, they had clashed over mares, and they had argued in the tribal council. Huvaz had no love for Duuron. Anyone else would see this elimination of a rival as a positive thing.

Not Huvaz. All he knew was that one of his tribe had been killed. It mattered not that he had always hated Duuron. He was the Horse Prince, and his people were his *responsibility*. A life-debt was owed – a valuation of the fallen, required to support the dead stallion's dependents: wife-mares, child-foals, and aged forebearers.

Duuron had many dependants: three mares, two foals, three colts, and his aged dam. They would suffer without the mighty brave's provision. It fell to the Horse Prince to bring them recompense.

"Which way did the Gray Murderer go?" Huvaz asked his people. With tosses of their heads, they indicated Shaykosch's path. Immediately, the Horse Prince galloped off, even before his tired braves could join him or counsel against this folly.

The Horse Prince ran. Ran and ran and ran. Minutes stretched into hours, hours into days, until he finally caught up with the Gray One.

Shaykosch was terrorizing the Star-Strider's village of Triticum, eating their bread, pawing their daughters, and fouling their stores of grain. Why did the Enemy do such? It is a question for the philosophers.

While Huvaz had little love for the Twofoots (except, of course, for the Princess Shoalla), and had clashed with them in the past, he gritted his teeth in anger at the devastation of their village.

He trotted up to Shaykosch, and said only this, "You have slaughtered one of my tribe, Duuron the Strong, and you must pay his life-debt: ten blankets of good wool, and five bushels of red oats. Else we must fight."

The Gray Wolf said "Go away, Pony Prince." And he took a single bite out of the granary, worth a season's amount of grain.

"Never," said Huvaz.

"So be it," said the Wolf, with a grin. He leapt at the Horse Prince, and the battle was joined.

They fought, teeth against fangs, hooves against claws. Sparks flew, blood ran. The battle raged for hours. Eventually, the Wolf stood triumphant over Huvaz.

"I spare you for your valor," said Shaykosch, panting. "None have ever danced with me so long. Go back to your people, Horse Prince, and be grateful for my mercy." And then the Gray Wolf loped off.

In this way, the Horse Prince saved the village of Triticum.

With pain and shame, Huvaz stood, blood streaming from his hide. Though he had driven the Enemy from Triticum, he had not triumphed against the beast. Without a word, without a thought, he followed the Wolf.

In Cuidad Llwynog, the city of the cunning Foxes, the Gray Wind had shifted his form into that of a Talking Rabbit, and was causing mischief among the Fox Guildsmasters (as was his wont). In this innocuous form, Shaykosch was auctioning a "miraculous cowhide" – which he claimed engendered wealth, health, and romantic potency, and had offered sly proofs to this effect – to the highest bidder. The Foxes were at each others' throats over this artifact, and the Wolf quietly chuckled at the show.

Huvaz saw through the disguise; he was not fooled by this change of shape, for the scent of the Wolf's blood was deep in his flaring nostrils. While Huvaz had little love for the Foxes, and had clashed with them in the past, the Horse Prince trotted up to Shaykosch, and said only this, "You have slaughtered one of my tribe, Duuron the Strong, and you must pay his life-debt: ten blankets of good wool, and five bushels of red oats. Else we must fight."

Shocked out of his evil plan, Shaykosch resumed his usual lupine form. "You, Huvaz," said Shaykosch, "are too stupid to live." Then, fangs glinting in the moonlight, he charged the Horse Prince.

They fought, teeth against fangs, hooves against claws. Sparks flew, blood ran. The battle raged for days. In the end, again Shaykosch stood triumphant over the Horse Prince, who lay bleeding, his throat torn by the sharper-than-sharp fangs of the Enemy.

"You did not have to die like this, brave one," said Shaykosch, panting heavily with his tongue lolling out. "It was your own fault. You should have just died, like a normal horse." Again, the Gray Wind left, ending his intrigues among the Foxes, to cause more mischief elsewhere.

In this way, the Horse Prince saved Cuidad Llwynog.

Again, in great pain and weakened from loss of blood, Huvaz forced himself to stand, bearing his grievous wounds. Though he had driven the Enemy from Cuidad Llwynog, he had not triumphed against the beast. Without a word, without a thought, he followed Shaykosch.

In Carabas, the Gray Wolf came to destroy the Purple Bridge that spanned the chasm of the Rushing River, connecting the kingdom of Giallo to that of Viola. As the Enemy snarled at the pathetic guardsmen upon the Bridge, he heard hoofbeats approaching from behind. Turning, he saw the Horse Prince bearing down on him, bleeding profusely, with a fiery rage in his eyes, smoke pouring from his flared nostrils.

"No!" cried the Enemy. "You should be dead!" For the first time in many years, fear touched the Wolf's cold, cold heart.

Huvaz trotted slowly up to Shaykosch, and said only this, "You have slaughtered one of my tribe, Duuron the Strong, and you must pay his life-debt: ten blankets of good wool, and five bushels of red oats. Else we must fight."

"Die!" growled the Enemy, and for the third time, the Gray Wolf and the Horse Prince clashed.

They fought, teeth against fangs, hooves against claws. Sparks flew, blood ran.

This time, Huvaz had the better: his sharp hooves cut into Shaykosch's flesh, tore off an ear, and trampled him down into the mud. Tons of weight against the Wolf's form. Kicks like lightning against ribs, legs, head. The Horse Prince could not be stopped, and the previous melees had taken more out of the Gray Wind's mettle than could be expected.

So, this time was *different*.

This time, Huvaz had the better of Shaykosch. The Horse Prince's amazing fortitude, his inability to quit, his sheer stubbornness – all these were weapons against the Gray Wind. No matter how the Wolf shifted shape, no matter what spells he cast, no matter what stratagems he employed, Shaykosch could not beat down Huvaz. The Horse Prince *endured*.

Huvaz fought on when most beings would lie down and die. He fought through pain, through fatigue, through hopelessness. He would not quit, or else his people would not have justice.

The battle raged for *weeks*, over the broken plains of Giallo. The Horse Prince refused to bow, to quit, to die, because not only had he been slighted by the murder of Duuron (his old foe, yet part of his people) and the refusal to pay the cost of such a death, but now he was *_furious_* with the Wolf.

Meanwhile, the Wolf – Murder on Three and a Half Legs (Huvaz had broken – nay, almost severed one!) – weakened; too far away from the cold and dark that would restore him. And the Horse Prince took the advantage.

Beaten bloody as he was, Huvaz soldiered through. Some say it was the rightness of his cause that empowered him to continue. Some say it was rage. Some say he was just basically super-tough.

They're all wrong.

We'll never know the answer; it might partake of some or all of these, but there is the whiff of an indefinable something that permeates the situation. The Horse Prince is too complex for simple answers.

With his heroic gifts of determination and tenacity, Huvaz eventually trampled Shaykosch down into the mud of Giallo. The piteous howls of the Wolf made no impression on the Horse Prince. When all of the pieces and parts of Shaykosch lay still,

Huvaz said only this: "The blood-debt is avenged."

In this way, the Horse Prince saved Carabas and the Purple Bridge.

Then, using his sharp hooves, he flensed the Wolf's hide from his body, and wore it as a bloody cape.

Gravely wounded, the Horse Prince turned his hooves homeward. The adventure he encountered on the way back. . . well, that's another tale.

THE END

The Taler's Truth

by Michaelbrent Collings

Once Upon A Time, in the Land of Zo. . .

Everyone knows that Zo is a thing of five parts (much like the broken China-Fairy of the Stone Bridge, though that is another tale). There is *Azul* in the East, *Giallo* in the West. *Rosso* stands to the south, and *Viola* rides at the northernmost crown of Zo.

Zo Proper is, of course, in the center. Everyone knows this, just as everyone knows that the sky is blue (except above Zink, where it is never other than a deep orange), the sun rises in the East (except on Roundabouts, when Giallo's royal bloodlines all come together and lasso her and pull her to them so that they may enjoy the bright sunrise over their yellow lands), and that the Great Jack is really rather a Mediocre Jack.

Everyone knows these things. There is much to know about Zo, and much that is to be known actually *is* known... at least by those who care to know.

But there are some things that are less well known, and others still less, and a few that are so unknown that it can be said that no one even knows how unknown they are.

Zo Himself/Herself/Itself fits into the middle of these categories. He/she/it is an enigma, a conundrum, and a riddle wrapped together and bound up with the twine of Myth. But the Zorcerer of Zo is not the only less-known thing.

Another is Plume.

Plume is part of the land of Zo, but it is not part of any of the *parts* of Zo. It is not in Azul, Giallo, Rosso, Viola, or even Zo Proper. And yet... and yet... nor is it apart from them, either.

Plume, it is said, was once a sixth part of the land of Zo. And where Azul grows wood, Giallo raises grain, and each of the other parts have their own particular specialties, Plume was famous for one thing only: Men and Women of Courage.

This is why, when the Gray Wolf Shaykosch first came to Zo, he immediately knew that he must deal with those men and women. For an unarmed child of Plume could destroy all but the greatest soldiers, a sickly woman with a spear could bring all but the greatest Sorcerers to their knees (if they had knees to be brought to), and the strongest warriors of Plume were a match even (it was whispered) for the great Zorcerer of Zo.

Death on Four Legs moved slowly for once. No gnashing of the teeth, no headlong attacks. He watched. He stalked. He bided his time.

When his move came, it was devastating. No one speaks of what happened – it is not even a matter of being another story, but rather a fact that those who spoke of it were also murdered in their beds. And stories, like Truth, must be repeated to survive. So now, untold years later, there is no story, there is no understanding of what happened to Plume lo those many years ago... and there is nearly no Plume.

The only way Plume survived after it lost its many Men and Women of Courage, was to *move*.

It did not move in the sense that its remaining people went to another place. What would that do? The Gray Beast of the Deathtime Sun would only find them there. No, they could not merely change *addresses*. They *moved*.

So one day the people of the lands bordering Plume came upon a great and empty field of barren rock where there had once been Mighty Cities and Thundering Castles and Vasty Keeps. Plume had moved. Occasionally sailors from Rosso claim to see it, shimmering like a Myrage of the Djinn, floating on the waters just over the horizon. Every now and then a Violan miner will come up after digging deep for Trill Gems and will swear he heard Plume's old battle songs coming from somewhere far in the ground below him. Uncommonly one of the Petty Tyrants and Corpulent Bureaucrats who claim to actually run Zo Proper (though this they only say when they have heard Zo Himself/Herself/Itself is away) will come out of one of the high towers and ask who approved zoning of a new city across the Rushing River, and why didn't they fill out the proper forms in decimoseptuplicate?

But no one ever notices Plume twice. It is forever on the run from the Gray Beast, forever moving. Ever glimpsed, but never actually *seen*.

The only people who *do* know where Plume is are the people within the land itself. And they are no longer Men and Women of Courage, but rather of necessity a Flighty Lot, and so are often hardly sure themselves where or even when they are.

One of the people of Plume was a Boy. His name was Weatheringfallhaffinstaff, a name far too grand for an orphan who was in charge of cleaning at the village inn. So everyone called him Chunkyalunkmunkchunkatunk, or Joe for short.

On one day, the day of this particular tale, Joe was busy cleaning. He always cleaned, he was always busy. But this day was worse than most. Plume had *moved* again, and in so doing had passed through a Hurrinado, a Twisty of the Highest Order. Much destruction had occurred, especially to larger buildings like the inn. The inn's owner, a gaunt Talking Weasel named Pheathar, had told Joe to have the common rooms cleaned, straightened, and spic-and-span by dinner or he would be beaten.

Joe knew he was likely to be beaten, because the common rooms had not merely been damaged, not simply been destroyed… they had been *carried away* in their entirety by the Gobsmack of a Swirl, along with five guests who had been eating dinner at the time.

Three of those guests had not yet paid their bills, which probably explained why Pheathar was in such a foul temper. Nothing irks a Weasel so much as providing a service for free.

So Joe saw a beating in his future, but he saw no point to sitting and crying all day. He got to work. He started early, with the sun still low in the Western Sky (it was Roundabouts time), and soon had taken off his shirt and was sweating freely in the warm air.

He built a door first. He was, after all, the child of an inn, so he knew that nothing makes people want to come in – and pay for the privilege – quite so much as a firmly closed door. The door was fine and sturdy, though it did look a bit odd standing in the dirt all alone, with no walls to either side, no floor behind and no porch before.

Someone knocked on the door.

Joe stared. He had had a clear view of his surroundings – the Lumbering WindTurner had ripped out not only the common rooms, but the surrounding forest and most of Pheathar's prize chicken-racing track (the losers were eaten by Pheathar himself on a regular basis) and had not seen anyone approach.

The knock came again.

"Hello?" Joe finally said. He thought it odd that the person –
whoever he/she/it was – should not simply walk around the
door.

"May I come in?" asked a voice. It was soft and lulling, the kind of
voice that invited Trust.

At this, Pheathar's training took over and Joe's response was
automatic. "What have you to trade for shelter?"

"Not much. Perhaps some wares?"

"What do you do? What are you?"

"A Taler."

Joe frowned. "We haven't need for sewing. I've but one set of
clothes, and Pheathar prefers to be in his All-Together."

The soft voice from beyond the door chuckled in a longsuffering
way. "Not a tailor, a *Taler*. Not a mender of clothes, but a weaver
of words. Language is the loom, and truth the warp and woof."

Joe thought. He sighed. "I'm sorry, Taler. But my master will beat
me if I let you in. He has no truck for Truth."

"Of course not, he's a businessman," answered the Taler. "How
about this? What if the wanderer at your door were to offer to
help you with your task?"

At that Joe threw the door open and shouted, "Enter, please, good
guest."

The Taler did as bidden. He (for Joe assumed it was a he) was
dressed top to bottom in a long cloak that covered all but his
fingers. The cloak was black, but seemed white because it was
covered with letters that had been stitched in silvery thread onto
every single space of its surface.

"What do those words say?" asked Joe (he could not read;

Pheathar did not like people reading because that almost always led to thinking Deep Thoughts and from there it was only a short skip to Independence and Trouble).

"Stories," answered the Taler. "But not of the type you are prepared for."

The Taler's fingers reached out and grasped a pair of rocks. He dragged them over to a line that Joe had scratched in the dirt, and placed them one atop the other. "Is this right?" he said.

Joe nodded. "That's a good start for the west wall," he said. He pointed to a mound of small boulders nearby. "There are more rocks over there." Then he turned and surveyed the emptiness that had once held walls and floors and ceilings and people, wondering what to do next.

"Have you heard the Tale of the Twice-Bitten Pigs?" asked the Taler, huffing a bit from within the folds of his cloak as he dragged two more rocks over to the wall he had started.

"I thought you were just going to help build," said Joe.

The Taler's shoulders bounced up and down in a quick shrug. "If a Taler does not speak stories, then what good can that Taler be?"

Joe smiled. He picked up a long piece of wood that might make a good central pillar for the room. "Tell me the tale, Taler."

They worked together that morning, that afternoon. Neither stopped, and Joe was amazed at his new companion's steady pace. Joe himself never let up, never ceased his work. But he had never before found someone who could keep pace with his efforts, either. And all the while, the Taler spoke tales of Might and Magic, of Mystery and Malice.

He told the Tale of Pixy Thistle, who went up the mountain to court the sun, and when he held the sun in his embrace he exploded into embers that became the stars.

He recited the Story of Jealous Falls, the watery sprite who hated one of the nearby village girls so much that she tried to cast herself off a mountainside and die to spite the girl. But the village girl (a genuinely Good Person) saved the sprite by casting a spell that held the jealous creature in the air, forever falling yet never hitting the bottom of the ravine, spilling tears of rage that formed a great, frothing lake below because she had been saved by an enemy and was forever in her debt.

He spoke the Fable of Kilarny, the girl who loved and lost and so decided never to love again so she could never again be hurt. But of course in doing so she found she had nothing to think of *except* her losses and now she wandered in agony through the Misty Moors, moaning in pain and looking for happiness to destroy.

And, of course, the stories eventually turned (as always they must) to the Zorcerer of Zo.

"What story of the Great Zo would you like to hear?" asked the Taler when Joe finally asked. The common room was coming along much faster with two working at it, but the boy still worried about the beating he knew was coming.

"Tell me the story of the Bottomless Chasm," said Joe.

The Taler paused a moment. "What?" he asked.

Joe didn't stop his work. The chimney was almost done. "The Bottomless Chasm, the story of the people who defied Zo, and so he turned their land into a hole so deep it goes through the world and comes out into the Backside of Nothing."

Joe's voice grew animated. He loved stories of Zo. That was why he didn't notice that the Taler had finally stopped working. The man's head (or where his head should be, under the cloak's hood) shook back and forth, and a loud sigh issued forth.

"So wrong," said the Taler. And he went back to work in silence.

The silence lasted only a few moments, though, and then he told his last Tale:

*   *   *

There once was a village called Naught. It was not called this because it was in any wise of Rude or Mean Circumstance. Rather the opposite. Naught was one of the richest places in Zo, rivaling even the Jade City for its opulence. But its people were haughty, and cloistered themselves away in their wealth. They allowed no one past their walls, permitted no visitor into their gates unless he was of equal or greater wealth than themselves. This never happened. Only Zo Himself/Herself/Itself might possibly possess such lucre.

One day a man appeared at their gates. He was wild in appearance, with sticks and brambles clinging to his hair, and a pair of carrion birds nesting in his gnarled beard. His teeth were bleeding, his eyes were crazed.

"Let me in," he shouted.

The guards at the gate merely laughed and did not even deign to reply.

The man laughed back. And this gave them pause. Moreso when he shifted and changed and revealed his true form: that of the Shaykosch, Gray Beast, Death on Four Legs. The deadly wolf growled at them. "I wished only to see the riches I have heard of," he said.

And when he said it there was something in his eyes that no one had ever seen. Tragedy. Because for this one moment, perhaps the only moment in Shaykosch's life, he had not sought violence or vengeance. He had heard of wealth in such measure as to defy belief, of art and artifacts so divine that they could call a soul out of Heaven. Yes, he had heard this last, and for a moment had pondered the possibility of capturing such a soul. Of possessing it for himself, and carrying it within him, and perhaps – just perhaps – becoming more than mere Beast.

He had fancied himself, for the barest instant, as a thing that might one day be, if not Good, then at the very least Better.

But the people of Naught had *laughed*. And nothing makes evil's hate burn so brightly as scorn.

The guards sounded the alarm and the city garrison formed, each man terrified of what the Deathless Wolf would do.

But Shaykosch did nothing. Just turned and padded away into the lengthening shadows of the day.

The guards smiled. They had frightened off the Immortal One! Even Death on Four Legs cowered before the riches of Naught.

Little did they know....

The next day, every man, woman, and child of Naught awoke to find themselves in a separate pit dug by the quick claws of Shaykosch. The wolf had himself once been caught in a pit dug by the Handsome Hunter (that's another tale…), and he knew how frightening such a thing can be. But, being the Beast he was, he had added his own personal touch to the trap.

Each man in his pit, each woman in her shaft, all the children in their own individual wells, saw the ground crumbling beneath their feet. The wolf had enchanted the earth, so that it would fall away below them.

They screamed. They screamed a scream such as has never been heard before or since in Zo. And when at last they finished, they heard the low, rumbling chuckle of Shaykosch. "You'll fall forever," he said. "Forever and ever, and I think that just. You will understand then what it was you turned away from your gates. You will comprehend the perfection of an Eternal Fall, and so will know me. And will suffer for it."

He laughed, and then ran away.

The pits continued crumbling, growing deeper and deeper. So deep that even the sun no longer reached the people in their oubliettes.

Then: a sound!

The Heroes of Zo!

They had come to save the people of Naught!

Here at one pit was The Blue Tailor, stitching with whip-quick turns of his nimble fingers, binding the very earth together so that the pit he watched would not crumble to eternity, so that he could stabilize it and save the man in its depths.

At another: Huvaz the Horse Prince, knocking at the sides of one of the forever-collapsing pits. He kicked with his steadfast horse legs, kicked and kicked and kicked with the tenacity that only Huvaz possesses. His hooves chipped, his bones broke, but he never stopped or faltered. He would not cease until he had knocked down enough dirt that the child at the bottom of his pit could climb atop it and escape.

To the cliff-edge of a third pit ran The Gingerbread Knight, and used his great strength to lower his friend Salt McTaffy down, down, down over the side. Salt McTaffy stretched and stretched and stretched, reaching for the woman below him.

They came. They all came.

And still, it was not enough. Not nearly enough. Each Hero struggled to reach but a single person. While thousands fell to Infinity around them.

Worse, the pits had crumbled so much that the very

Underpinnings of Zo were giving way. The pits were coming together to form a great –

["Bottomless Chasm!" shouted Joe, knocking over the half-finished table he was building in his excitement.

"Yes, yes, yes," said the Taler, sounding more than a trifle irritated. "Are *you* going to tell the rest of the story?"

"Sorry," said Joe.]

– Bottomless Chasm. A chasm deeper than Deep, a drop that would remind those who plummeted to its reaches what it was like to be Doomed and Damned. That would teach them what it was to be the Gray Beast.

The Heroes despaired. They did not know if they would save a single person each. And they *did* know that the others were all doomed.

They despaired, yes, but at the same time they each nurtured an ember of hope in the ashes of their attempts to save. The spark that was the Zorcerer of Zo.

And at the moment of their greatest discouragement, the moment when hopelessness threatened to drag the Heroes down into chasms no less deep than the ones swallowing Naught, someone – or some*thing* – appeared in the ruins of the city.

A specter, a ghost. A wizard, a wraith.

Each person of Naught, deep in his or her pit, heard the same thing in turn. Each heard the same voice. A voice neither man nor woman, neither Human nor Animal.

"Are you alive, good Naughtian?" said Zo.

"Save me!" they each cried. And then saw something coming.

Something strange and writhing like a snake.

A rope.

The rope dropped to them. At first each citizen of Naught despaired. The ground was crumbling at their feet, they would soon fall into the Great Dark that is found Below All. The rope could not possibly reach.

But... it *did*. And each man, woman, and child of Naught realized that the rope was magic. It was growing so that it would always be just within their grasp.

"Hold tight and climb the rope!" shouted Zo, unseen above them.

Each person in turn reached for the rope dropped by the Zorcerer.

And each person in turn... *did not take hold*.

"Save me!" they each shouted. "Don't make me climb the rope, just use your magic to save me now."

"We cannot," came Zo's voice. "There is no time for us to work such spells for each of you. We have given you the means to save yourselves. Now climb!"

Then there would be nothing. Zo had moved to the next person in despair, had run to drop a Saving Thread to the next life in threat.

Every person was given a rope. Every person was asked to climb.

And every person – *every. single. person.* – refused to do so, secure in the knowledge that surely Zo would, had to, *must* pull them up Himself/Herself/Itself.

Soon the pits joined.

Soon the Bottomless Chasm opened up and swallowed Naught.

The Heroes did their work. They escaped, and with them each carried a single citizen of Naught. Perhaps a barrelmaker's dozen survivors.

And what happened next? Did those survivors, those few angry wretches who had caused their own fall, condemn Shaykosch? Did they fault themselves? No. They blamed *Zo*.

"He punished us," they told all who would listen, to the end of their days. "We didn't want to follow Him/Her/It, so He/She/It created the Bottomless Chasm and swallowed our fathers and mothers and sisters and brothers. Great and Terrible is Zo, and Merciless in His/Her/Its power."

The Blue Tailor saved a single man.

Huvaz the Horse Prince carried forth a sole child.

The Gingerbread Knight and Salt McTaffy together could only rescue one small (and rather cranky) woman.

For this – for one person each – they were revered and remembered as Heroes and Champions.

And Zo? All He/She/It did was provide the masses with the means to save themselves. So of course He/She/It was blamed forever after for their destruction.

And that, Boy, is the *True* Tale of the Bottomless Chasm.

*   *   *

Joe frowned. He was putting the finishing touches on the ceiling, hanging from a sling he had knit out of spidersilk blossoms while the Taler wove his account. But the ceiling seemed to disappear for a moment, to fall away from his sight just as the Bottomless Chasm must have fallen from the feet of the people of Naught.

"I don't think I like that version of the story as much as I do the other," he finally said.

The Taler, sitting below him and tap-tap-tapping individual floor tiles into place, sighed. "Of course you don't. Truth is never as pleasant as Lies. That's why Lies still exist, for what other purpose can they have but to please us? But it is the pleasure a fly feels when finally invited to dine with the spider. Such luxury, such silken comfort! And only when it is too late does the poor fly realize that the comfort was the trap, that the easy way was Death."

The Taler stood, and went to the door. The door was now held snugly within two walls – walls that must have been built while the story had been told, though Joe could not for the life of him remember if *he* had built the walls, or if they had been constructed by the Taler.

The cloaked man reached out, and grasped the door handle. Joe realized for the first time that the Taler's hands were more like those of a sprite than those of a human. Or were they more like a man's? A woman's? Something else?

What is happening? he thought.

The Taler pulled open the door.

"Wait," shouted Joe, suddenly anxious for his new companion not to leave. "You said you'd help me finish the rooms!"

The Taler's head swept left and right, clearly taking in the surroundings from within the depths of the hood. "That was payment for one person staying at the inn. But none shall stay today, and this Taler shall move on."

"Why?"

"Others need to hear this. Need to hear the Tales and Truths."

"*I* need you," Joe half-screamed. "I'll be beaten!"

The Taler's head shook with whisper-soft rustles of fabric. "No. Not if you hurry and finish. You've had enough help to get the job done in time. But only just enough. So don't dawdle."

The Taler stepped out the door.

"Wait!" Joe shouted again. The Taler paused. "You never even told me your name."

"Name?" The Taler's low, silky voice issued from the depths of the hood. Joe could not now – and never had – seen the Taler's face. "What is a name, Joe? As you well know, a name is just a thing that people call you as shorthand for all that you are. As for *our* name...." The Taler stepped away, and seemed to fade from view like a dream upon waking.

"... well, that's another tale."

THE END

The Witch Girl

by Chad Underkoffler

For Gwyn

Once Upon A Time, in the Land of Zo. . .

There was a kingdom called Viola, high in the northern mountains. It was a magical land – even more magical than the rest of Zo! – chock full of witches, goblins, Talking Animals, Living Toys, winged monkeys, dragons, and all other sorts of strange and wonderful creatures.

To Viola came a girl from one of the innumerable Otherworlds that kiss the boundaries of Zo – a young girl, wearing tiny glasses in rectangular frames. This was Theodora. Like all Otherworlders, there were signs that marked her apart from the (human) inhabitants of Zo. Two signs, in fact: 1) her hair was stark, brilliant white, so much so it even glowed; and 2) she never aged, in all the years she spent wandering the hills and valleys of Viola. This is not to say that she didn't learn or gain in knowledge, skill, and power; it was just that her body simply did not grow up. She remained a child.

As Otherworlders are wont to do in the Zantabulous Land of Zo, Theodora had adventures where she learned truths, made friends and enemies, and served as the fulfillment of prophecy then and anon. And she studied –– studied like no Otherworlder had before or since. Her passion? *Magic*.

She served her apprenticeship in the Gingerbread Cottage of Goodwife Sweetinbargendol – more commonly known as "Goody Sweet." There she learned the basics of witchery (brooms, curses, herbs, and such), and first gained her epithet "the Witch Girl." Alas, her mystical talents did not lie along the same lines of Goody Sweet's Confectionary Magic. (Also, Goody Sweet disapproved of Theodora's volatile and vengeful temperament.) Eventually, Theodora's apprenticeship ended, and she left the Gingerbread Cottage.

She aided the Crows of Snowtop Peak – crows in Zo, you must know, at this time had snow-white plumage! – in their war against the Vultures of the Pancake Plain. During that time, she gained the friendship, trust, and love of one of their kind: Mnemosyne, the Crow Princess. When Theodora left Snowtop, Mnemosyne accompanied her as her familiar.

The Witch Girl learned grammarye from Skychom the Syntactic, and began delving into the True and Universal Names of things. She traveled with the nomadic Whyggles along Four Shays Road, becoming steeped in their mysteries, like how to step "sideways" and find a new path to her destination. She studied the crystal-magic of the Adamants, listening to their chatter and smelling their aromas, nose and ear pressed against their invulnerable diamond anthills, learning the secrets of minerals – dull rock and gemstone alike. She was educated in gematria by the Unorthodox Rabbit, prosodigitations by the Go-et Poet (and his twin brother, the Goat Poat) of Middlevale, rhymancy by Verisifer Jones, rune-lore by Ragnar the Mad, and spellingcraft by the King Bee of Castle Hive.

Interspersed with her studies, Theodora rescued the children of Smitwiggle from the Mad Piper, freed the Turtle Prince of his dire curse, cursed the Squire of Breezedale for his villainy, crushed the Goblin army that threatened Bugburg, and drummed the Copperdoodles out of Timpani. In short, she had a busy few years.

After ending the Rule of the Dreadful Doog, Theodora the Witch Girl decided to settle down. Tired of scaling rough and ready passes, this hardy little lass's only desire was to rest, preferably somewhere on the shore. She came to Shell Beach, on the northern coast of Viola, and there built her home: Turtle Tower.

(Shell Beach, of course, was named for the great stone shells that littered its sands, the only remnant of the Thunder Turtles that ruled the Land of Zo in the long ago. Theodora, with her arts, used these shells to build her fastness: Turtle Tower – turtle shells all the way up!)

After making herself comfortable at Turtle Tower, Theodora dedicated herself to her sabbatical from adventuring. She played her favorite games, read innumerable books, counted stars by candlelight, wrote poetry, and even (occasionally) taught the youth of the town their letters. After risking the uncertain pains of adventuring, she was glad of the rest.

One night, while playing at scramble-rune with Mnemosyne at the top of Turtle Tower in the spring air and bright moonlight, the Witch Girl had a vision. Just as the white crow princess was about to place a runestone (for a quintuple word score!), the Witch Girl threw up her hand to stop the play. "Wait!" said Theodora. "There is a message here."

She studied the grid. In play were HOARY, CHESS, and SHEIK.

In the arcane depths of her mind, these runestones resolved into an anagram, an ominous message: SHAYKOSCH IS HERE. Inadvertently, she shuddered in horror.

Shaykosch! The Deathless Wolf. The Gray Wind. Murder-on-Four-Legs. The Adversary. Always against the Zorcerer, always out to rule the Empire of Zo. A being of evil, pain, and mocking laughter.

A bell began to ring from far below, signaling a supplicant come to see the Witch Girl.

"This bodes not well," said Theodora, rising from the game. Mnemosyne shrugged, and flitted along.

Down in the Audience Chamber (composed of a single Thunder Turtle Shell of vast proportions), stood a visitor: a young boy, armed with shield and sword. He wore no helmet, and displayed the same sort of glowing white hair as Theodora.

As she entered, he bowed gracefully. "Theodora the Witch Girl! I am Jack, an Otherworlder like yourself, in the service of a great lord who stands against tyranny! I come to beg alliance between you and my master."

Theodora crossed her arms, and flatly examined the boy. For a time, she said nothing. Then, with great scorn, she replied, "I name you 'Jack Wolf.' You are Shaykosch, come to gain my aid in your war against the Zorcerer." Mnemosyne fluttered, shedding a few snowy feathers in shock and fear.

The boy smiled, and his shape began to melt. "I should have known better than to play with such an insightful girl as you," he said, growing hairier, larger. In moments, a great gray wolf sat on its haunches across the chamber from Theodora. "Even so, I do desire your aid against the Tyrant."

The Witch Girl stared impassively at the Gray Wolf. "The Zorcerer has done naught to me," she said. "Indeed, his rule from the Jade

Throne seems to have eased the travails of all the kingdoms of Zo." She smiled a small smile. "Therefore, I shall not ally with you, Shaykosch."

The Wolf grew angry, fury turning his eyes a shining red. "You Good Witches are all alike," he slavered. "Afraid of your power. Afraid to rule. Afraid to crush your enemies."

At this, Theodora merely laughed. "You may go," she said, offering a dismissive gesture with her hand as she turned away from him, to take the stairs back to the tower-top.

This was a mistake.

A mistake, because she did not see the shifting form of Shaykosch. His fur retreated and hardened into scales. His neck lengthened. Batwings budded from his shoulders. The Wolf became a Dragon.

"If you will not aid me, you will burn!" cried the transformed Shaykosch, and he exhaled a gout of fire towards Theodora's unprotected back!

"No!" cried Mnemosyne, Theodora's companion and familiar. She flew, interposing herself between the Wolf-Dragon's fiery attack and the body of her friend.

Dragonflame consumed the Crow Princess, charring her, setting her plumage alight. She screamed in her agony.

Theodora turned and saw the flaming body of her friend. A murderous fury lit her eyes, and her glasses could not minimize this wrath; her pupils glowed red-hot with rage.

"Presitidigitalis!" she cried at the Wolf-Dragon – this was a magical curse used to explode the heart of a foe.

Indeed, Shaykosch's heart exploded. He flailed momentarily on the chamber floor.

Meanwhile, Theodora employed her most puissant healing charms to stabilize Mnemosyne. Although her friend's feathers still smoked, her snowy-white plumage charred to black, the Crow Princess yet lived. Theodora laid on her most impressive enchantments to preserve the life of her friend.

Thus engaged, it came as a shock when the burbling voice of Shaykosch came from behind her. "I am undying. Detonating my heart is not enough, girl. I am the Deathless Wolf!"

Theodora, her recuperative charms complete, turned back to face Shaykosch, who was rising from the flagstone floor of the Audience Chamber. "Let us see how 'deathless' you are, beast. "

She spoke the words of Winter Discontent, sending a spray of magic intended to freeze the marrow in the Wolf's very bones. The blue energy snapped and crackled as it approached its target.

Who, in the meanwhile, did nothing. He merely growled – and the vibration of his call shattered Theodora's spell. "I am the soul of Winter," he laughed. "Simple curses of frost and snow have no effect on me!" And then he began to inhale a vast amount of air.

"I am the Winter Wind," cried, Shaykosch. "Feel my chilling wrath!" And then the wolf blew, an Arctic stream of cold-death. Houses, even castles entire, had been shattered and scattered by the Wolf's blowing.

Not so with the Turtle Tower. For Theodora the Witch Girl, through her mystical arts, changed Shaykosch's WIND to WAND. The winds entire coalesced and calmed, forming in Theodora's hand a silver wand: the *Wand of the Winds*. This, of course, denied the Wolf access to his most trenchant power forevermore.

Back and forth the magical battle raged. The Wolf and the Witch Girl were evenly matched.

For hours – some say days! – the battle raged. Shifting shapes and potent magics shocked the countryside. Spell met counterspell, and counter-counterspell.

Theodora wiped the sweat from her brow. What could be done against a foe that – at the very least – could change his form into something resistant to magical attack? As the Wolf became a fish, the inkling of an idea struck Theodora.

She said, "Shaykosch, your greatest strength is the fluidity of your form. So be it. I say, with the potency of the Semordilap Palidromes: *'FLOW WOLF!'*" These were the words of the Palindromic Prison, both prismatic and precise. There was no recourse.

Instantly, the shape of Shaykosch weakened and flowed. Affected by the Witch Girl's spell, his control over his shifting of shape was destroyed. Unable to control his form, the Wolf collapsed into a puddle of gray, furry goo. Affected by the Witch Girl's spell, the Gray Wind could not return to his wolf-shape. The furry goo roiled in anger.

Theodora laughed, and spoke the incantations of the Adamants to form a diamond-hard urn to contain the Wolf's fluid form. Then, she sealed the urn with many arcane sigils of dire consequence.

Shaykosch was trapped. Theodora had won. The land of Zo was safe from the Gray Wind's depredations for a time.

Mnemosyne – who had recovered from the dragon-flame, though (alas!) her plumage was now charred and inky black – placed the Adamantine Urn on the topmost spire of Razor Peak, just for safekeeping. (This was, of course, at Theodora's direction.) If the Wolf broke free, he would slice himself into pieces upon the mountain's blood-keen sides; the deadliness of ascent would preclude his minions from attempting a rescue.

In a form of encomium for their brave and stalwart princess, the Crows of Zo deliberately altered their white feathers for black. This they did to honor the best of birds, the companion of the Witch Girl. Theodora herself used her arts to exchange her glowing white hair for glowing black hair of deepest sable.

For many years after this event, Viola was at peace.

Unfortunately, there are always rats seeking to hook their wagon to an evil star. Many years after Theodora returned to her Otherworld, the Wolf was freed. How Shaykosch escaped the Witch Girl's prison, and regained his wind... well, that's another tale.

THE END

The Ship-Breaker

by Andrew Byers

Once Upon A Time, in the Land of Zo. . .

The land of Rosso was sick. Well, to be more accurate, the people of Rosso were sick. Very badly sick, with a strange illness that had never been seen before. It came to be called the Scarlet Plague, as it turned its victims that color before killing them, and none of Rosso's physicians could cure it. All was not lost, however. The many alchemists and healers of the land of Viola assembled and set out to discover a cure for the Scarlet Plague. For many days and many nights, they labored over the cure, while the people (and Talking Animals) of Rosso grew sicker and sicker. Some – nay, *many*! – in Zo began to despair that a cure might ever be discovered. Eventually, a remedy that combined medicine and magic was found. This lavender elixir was made from crushed elderberries and nightingale songs and the roots of mountains and many other things best not to recount here, and it tasted vile, as all the best medicine does.

Time was of the essence, so the medicine was loaded into casks and placed in the hold of a deep-bellied carrack named *Zolion's Grace* and sent out to sea to make the ocean voyage to Port

Carmine, the capital of Rosso.

There was just one problem, however. Recently, the coasts of Rosso had been subject to sudden and mysterious storms and fogbanks that had led to a number of ships crashing against the rocky coastline, their crews and cargos lost to the sea. Was there some kind of ship-breaker at work? Was it simple bad luck? This was a particularly bad problem for a maritime nation like Rosso, and if the situation were not already overshadowed by the Scarlet Plague, would have been a matter of great import. But now that the *Zolion's Grace* – and its precious cargo – risked a similar fate as it neared Rosso, it became a matter of supreme urgency.

So, a very special envoy of the Zorcerer of Zo, a hero in his own right named Horace Hogg, fourth and youngest of the Hogg brothers, was dispatched to precede the *Zolion's Grace* and see what could be done to ensure its safe passage to Port Carmine. If some nefarious plot was afoot – the work of a ship-breaker perhaps? – he was to root it out; if the shipwrecks were caused by ill luck, then Horace would likewise see what he could do to smooth the way.

Horace Hogg, Esquire, was – first and foremost – a gentleman. He was also an enchanter and swordsman of no small renown. Horace was no stranger to adventure, or heroism, or danger, having defeated the Deathless Wolf once before, with his friend Deril, a talking crocodile with an unusual belly (take my word for it). Since then, he had negotiated a treaty with the Hob-Knobblers, trounced the Black Badger of Bramblecorn, and even found the Lost Isles of Lenore (and then lost them again, but we can't hold that against him).

Horace anticipated no problems he couldn't handle in Rosso, but was wary, for strange things were afoot. He traveled overland with all due haste because he knew that he had only a short while before the ship approached the Rosson shoreline on which so many other ships had recently been shattered. As night fell, Horace began to grow anxious. Not only had he not yet uncovered any possible causes of the mysterious storms and fog, neither had he determined how or why ships might be driven against the rocky coast during these storms, nor what might have happened to the wrecked ships' crews or cargoes. Horace's keen eyes, sharp wit, and magical investigations had all thus far failed him. Horace – as both a gentleman and a pig of hearty appetite – wondered if he would be forced to once again camp outdoors and eat the less than appetizing food he had stored in his travel satchel. A grey drizzle began to fall and Horace was a miserable pig indeed.

That is why the slightly ramshackle manor house on the edge of the clifftop overlooking the sea looked so appealing. At first glance, the place appeared empty, but as he got closer Horace could see a few dim lights in some of the windows and caught the faint whiff of smoke from one of the manor's chimneys. No one stirred, but Horace marched up to the front door and gave the bell cord a long pull.

Then another.

He waited a few minutes, then gave another long pull. He could faintly hear the bell as he rang it, but still no one stirred.

Horace began rapping on the door with his walking stick.

After a long time, he could hear footsteps approach, then a series of locks were disengaged. Eventually the door was opened a crack and a surly voice bellowed "What do you want?"

Taken aback, Horace replied "First, sir, the common courtesy due any weary traveler. Second, I would like to request shelter for the night from the storm that is brewing. I will not be able to make it to town before the storm breaks. Third, well, if you could provide a traveler with a light supper, I would be most appreciative."

Taken aback, the voice said incredulously, "That's all?"

"Yes," Horace said, pushing his way into the manor with one meaty shoulder. Sometimes a gentleman must know when to be assertive. "Don't worry, I'm not a finicky eater; I am happy to share in whatever you may have on hand."

The ruffian at the door – and Horace made no mistake that the man dressed in stained livery was anything but a ruffian – was clearly nonplussed. After a long pause: "Welcome, then, to Vulpine Hall. I suppose."

Horace was grudgingly ushered into the main foyer of the manor house. The place was dimly lit and chilly. It had cobwebs in the corners and herds of dustbunnies rolled about freely in the hallways. As Horace was escorted to his bedchamber, they passed several other servants loitering about the place, including several disreputable-looking humans who wouldn't have looked out of place in a dockside tavern, an ocelot who hissed at Horace as he passed by, a pair of tittering ferrets, a hulking boar with a broken tusk, and a particularly grubby-looking muffin man who had a few bites taken out of his top and what appeared to be a missing eye lost in a knife fight. Scoundrels, one and all. Horace could tell. He didn't like the looks of this, not one bit.

After reluctantly placing his travel bag in the grimy bedchamber he was assigned – Horace double-checked that its lock was secure – he was brought to the manor's dining hall and seated at the great table, indifferently set. "The master will join you for dinner. At some point." His guide left to attend to other duties (or loaf, more likely). Horace surreptitiously polished his silverware on a slightly stained napkin.

The meal, when it was eventually brought out, left something to be desired. While Horace was not what he would consider a gourmand – he tended to favor quantity over quality in his meals – he did not consider stale bread, wilted lettuce, and a burnt casserole of noodles and unidentified meat to constitute a delightful feast. Alas. His hopes for a good meal to sate his hunger fell with every course.

"Ah, Horace Hogg, we meet again," a sly and familiar voice called out from behind Horace.

Horace spun about to see who his host was. "Reynardo! A pleasure to see you again." The pig mustered a smile, though he was anything but joyous to see his old acquaintance, a fox named Reynardo, standing in the doorway.

The years had not served the fox well. Grey dotted his muzzle and someone had once taken a chunk out of Reynardo's left ear. He was wearing what had once been a fine emerald green velvet smoking jacket, but it was now covered in stains. Still, the fox gave Horace a toothy grin.

Horace did not have fond memories of his old college "chum," Reynardo. The two had been fellow students at Lime University in Jade City in Zo Proper many years previously. Reynardo had been an upperclassman when Horace was an underclassman. They were by no means friends; Reynardo had had a bad reputation and Horace had not wanted to associate with such a person. Once, the pig had had to stop Reynardo and a couple of his cronies from bullying a timid little fennec named Quimby. That had caused some trouble, but Horace had been in the right. Eventually, Reynardo had left the university under mysterious circumstances and they had not seen each other since.

The pair began a desultory conversation in which it was clear that neither party wished to reveal much about their current activities. Between bites of overcooked and mostly flavorless meat – that couldn't be pork, could it? – Horace noted a particular piece of jewelry worn on his host's breast. "That is an interesting pin you wear in your cravat, my friend," Horace said, though he liked not the looks of a silver wolf's head, which looked all too similar to the symbol of his old foe Shaykosch, the Deathless Wolf, who was defeated – for now – but not yet dead.

"You like it, my old schoolchum?" the fox grinned slyly. "An old friend gave it to me."

Horace didn't inquire further.

After dinner, it was clear that both Horace and Reynardo were happy to excuse themselves; each pleaded fatigue. A lizard man in faded livery and dungarees escorted Horace to the bedchamber that had been assigned to him. Once there, Horace threw the bolt securing the door and prepared for bed.

*   *   *

Horace was not paranoid, but he was cautious, and he *always* relied on his intuition. And since he had arrived at Vulpine Hall, his intuition had been *screaming* at him to depart. Or, failing that, to be very, very careful. Around midnight Horace knew that his intuition had once more saved his life when – from his vantage point under the bed – Horace spied two dark and husky forms slip out of a secret door in his bedchamber wall and creep over to the bed. Curious to see what they intended, Horace readied himself for action as they drew swords and, raising them above their heads, brought them down over and over again on the pillowy form Horace had fashioned under the bedcovers.

"That's not very sporting of them!" Horace thought to himself. Peeping out from under the bed, he waved his hands in mystic passes and gestured with a wand he held at the ready. The two thugs began to yawn uncontrollably. Their swords drooped at their sides. One turned to the other, saying "Is it just me or are you suddenly very . . . sleepy . . .?" Before the other goon could reply, both had crashed to the floor. Horace dragged himself out from under the bed, then quickly bound and gagged the men.

Time to see what was *what* here at Vulpine Hall. Horace readied satchel and swordcane and slipped into the secret passageway. Horace's wand glowed faintly from its tip, allowing him to navigate through the hidden corridor. The place was dusty but he could tell that many, many feet had recently trod through the area. Periodically he would happen upon peep holes and latches opening secret passages into various parts of the manor.

It occurred to Horace that he could use this network of secret doors and peepholes to surreptitiously scout out the manor when he spied a likely door through a peephole that clearly warranted further investigation. It was a stout door secured with thick iron bands and a multitude of locks. Casual visitors (or the fox's servants) were clearly not meant to venture inside. Horace rifled through his valise and withdrew a thin wand of yew, then slowly opened a secret door across the hallway from the mystery door. Making mystic gestures and muttering a few judicious phrases in the language of enchantment, the door's locks sprang open with a clatter and the door swung inward. He glanced around to see if anyone had heard the noise – it did not appear anyone was coming to investigate – and cautiously pushed the door open all the way.

An icy chill came upon Horace's capacious stomach as he saw what lay within the treasure room, for that was clearly what it was. Deep piles of gold and silver coins covered the floor in piles. Bolts of silk were stacked haphazardly in one corner, while another held racks of expensive oils, fragrances, spices, and indigo dye. Paintings and other *objets d'art* were jumbled crudely throughout. These were clearly the plundered treasures of the ships that had disappeared along the Rosson coastline. All uncertainty of Reynardo's involvement in the mystery dissipated.

Shaking his head, Horace left the treasure vault and relocked the door, knowing he could return the treasures to their rightful owners later. Horace crept back inside the secret corridor and made his way toward the back of the manor, where he knew Reynardo's bedchamber must be located. Finding a rich ebony door with expensive moldings soon thereafter, Horace knew he had found it. Once again, he magicked the door open.

There was little time to lose and after a quick glance inside the bedchamber, Horace knew that his quarry was not present. He turned to leave, but as he did, his eyes fell upon a curtained alcove. Warily, Horace approached and threw back the curtain, revealing a large silver-framed mirror. Or, at least, something *like* a mirror, for it did not reflect the bedchamber, nor could Horace see himself in its reflection. Instead it seemed to show some dimly-lit, shadowed area. Horace touched the frame and drew back his hand quickly – it was ice-cold. Horace realized he could see his breath, then shivered from the intense cold emanating from the mirror. He peered more closely into it. Was that slight movement in the distance? The shadows seemed to shift slowly. He began to feel as though he was being watched by . . . something. Dread and realization crept over him. With one quick gesture and a whispered word of magic – for Horace was no novice when it came to enchantment – he shattered the mirror with his walking stick. As the silvered pane of enchanted glass cascaded to the floor, Horace heard a faint, plaintive wolf's howl as though from very far off. He ground the broken glass under his trotters then prepared to slip into the hallway.

A slight scuff of a foot on the threadbare carpet and the scent of moldy muffin was all that alerted Horace to the hulking forms that awaited him on either side of the door. That disreputable-looking muffin man and the broken-toothed boar sprang at him. Horace leaped back into Reynardo's bedchamber just in time, the two thugs jostling each other to enter the room to dispatch the poor pig. They could only come into the room one at a time, and

Horace took advantage of that. He used his walking stick to sweep the boar's legs out from under him. The boar slammed into the floor with a resounding crash and Horace gently tapped him on the temple, sending the boar to slumberland. The ungainly muffin man tried – and failed – to scramble over the porcine heap in the doorway. That provided Horace the opportunity he needed to send a couple of quick jabs into the spongy noggin of his foe. Muffin crumbs falling like dandruff, he too collapsed on top of the boar.

Horace sighed and clambered over the goonish servants' unconscious forms.

He knew that he had to find Reynardo, who clearly was up to no good. In all these nocturnal travels, Horace had yet to spy the master of the house. Having given at least a cursory look over the manor, Horace cautiously approached the doorway to the central tower. That seemed the quickest way to the rooftop. Where else could Reynardo be in this supernatural storm?

When Horace threw back the trapdoor to the rooftop he was immediately buffeted by wind and rain. He could hear the sly tones of Reynardo speaking – chanting, more likely – off in the distance, but his gaze was drawn to a strange tower of wrought iron that had been erected on the highest point of the roof. It held a complicated mirror-like contraption that captured the light of the full moon and reflected it out to sea, churning up strange fogs upon the water. As Horace's gaze was drawn toward the light, he realized it was dancing and flashing and shifting across his vision, almost immediately giving him a splitting headache and making the world appear to spin.

Horace turned away before he could be hypnotized by its dancing light. It took a greater force of will than it should have to break his gaze. Anyone seeing the light would become disoriented, confused, bewildered. That certainly would wreak havoc on someone, say, trying to steer a ship at sea . . . .

As Horace considered the possibilities, a voice broke into his reverie. "Aha! I see I have an unwelcome visitor this night! Nasty little piglet, always poking his snout where it doesn't belong."

Horace's head jerked around. Drat! The fox had already spotted him. "Yes, indeed, Reynardo. I suspected you of much, and you didn't disappoint me," Horace said, gesturing toward the spindly tower and its eerie hypnotic light.

"Foolish meddler! This is none of your concern. You should have continued your travels and not sought the hospitality of Vulpine Hall tonight."

"On the contrary, Reynardo. My purpose in coming here was to locate the fiend behind the recent rash of ships being dashed upon the nearby shore. It was quite a mystery: why would otherwise skilled ship captains inadvertently steer their ships into rocks on a part of the coastline they must sail past every day? But I think I've discovered the reason why, haven't I, Reynardo?" Horace said with a significant glance toward the mirror.

The fox nodded ruefully. "Such a smart little piggie, aren't you? You know, I never did like you at university, Horace!"

"Believe me, the feeling was mutual."

Renardo laughed. "Oh, my fat little hog! I hope you don't think you have a chance in the world of stopping me, do you? I am skilled with blade and spell, and the Wolf will surely aid me. Why, I think I'll have some suckling pig for tomorrow's dinner! I will have much to celebrate, after all . . . ."

Such witty repartee could not continue forever, Horace knew. He had a villainous plot to stop, after all. The fox was clearly losing his patience anyway. As Reynardo drew his sword, Horace caught a glint from the ruby eyes of a wolf's head set in the fox's blade's pommel. "I knew I didn't care for that wolf's head cravat pin when I saw it at dinner! I've taken care of him once before, you might recall . . . ."

"I am not ashamed of the Mighty Wolf I serve, little pig! All that I do here, I do in His name! These treasures I loot from these ships will fund the mighty magics I need to return the Hungry One to life! And, I must admit, it gives me great satisfaction to know that the cure for the Scarlet Plague will soon be dumped into the sea!"

Horace shook his head. "Reynardo, you were always a bad egg, but do you really want to see innocents die for your master's sake? Is that the sort of creature you've become?"

"I don't care about 'innocents'! What are they to me? Shaykosch has enriched me beyond measure, pig. I do His will gladly. Let me show you some of what He has taught me!"

Reynardo snarled a magic word and a black python appeared, wrapped around Horace's neck. It began slowly *squeeeezing*, its tongue flicking at him as it did so. Horace could barely utter the word of counter-spell before his throat was crushed. The serpent disappeared, and in its place . . . "I would have preferred a cream ascot," as he adjusted his new ebon silk cravat (Horace having neglected to don the proper attire after surviving the assassination attempt earlier).

Seeing this, the fox waved his arms madly about and a swarm of chittering bats flew out of a sudden rent in the sky over Vulpine Hall, hurtling toward Horace Hogg. Just before they reached him, Horace waved his wand and the vampiric bats transformed into a cloud of butterflies. A very wet, bedraggled cloud of butterflies that quickly dispersed to seek shelter from the storm. Horace guiltily spat one of the little creatures out of his mouth and readied himself for the fox's next sorcerous stratagem.

Reynardo ground his teeth together and redoubled his efforts. He danced a frantic jig and waved his arms wildly in the air. The crack of thunder came from just above their heads and Horace only had a split second to raise his wand into the air and transform it into an umbrella tipped with a lightning rod that drew the lightning that Reynardo had summoned and harmlessly dissipated it.

"That tingled," Horace said.

The fox was now panting and his maniacal grin had turned sour.

"You have learned much since university, Reynardo."

"As have you, pig. Unfortunately," the fox replied through gritted fangs. "Enough magic for one night, Hogg. Let us see if you have learned anything of the martial, rather than magical, arts."

"I think you will find I have also attained some proficiency with the blade." And with that, the duel was on in earnest. Horace barely got his swordcane up in time to deflect the fox's wild slash. One would thrust. The other would parry, or dodge, or evade the blow using skill, ingenuity, or pure luck. Back and forth, back and forth they danced across the rain-slicked roof. They lunged, riposted, slashed, and leaped away just in time, again and again. Neither could gain an advantage over the other; they were just too evenly matched. Horace knew that time was not on his side. A draw would mean that, since the mirror-tower was still working its magic, eventually the medicine-bearing ship would be lured to its doom – a catastrophic defeat to be sure – and eventually the fox's remaining servants would appear to see what the rooftop clamoring was all about and help their leader overwhelm him.

Horace gathered his wits and steeled himself, for he knew that eventually he would tire – he could feel himself beginning to flag already – and that would mean he would grow sloppy, careless, and that could mean doom, perhaps even a long fall off the roof and an ignominious end to an otherwise promising life. Horace was not the only one beginning to tire, and Reynardo dropped his guard just a bit as they dueled across the rooftop. Was Reynardo luring him into a trap? Horace took a chance, lunged, tangled up

Reynardo's blade with his own and wrenched it out of the fox's hand. The fox panted in shock and horror at his disarming.

Rather than simply running him through, Horace bowed slightly and gestured, allowing Reynardo the opportunity to pick up his sword, which he quickly took. Horace's gentlemanly conduct was rewarded with a snarl and a lunge, which he parried neatly. The fox flew into a frenzy, seeming to give up defending himself and plunging into an all-out attack. He drove Horace back three feet, five feet, ten, then Horace was all the way across the roof, his back to the edge. It was all he could do to prevent himself from being skewered by the fox's all-out attacks.

Then Horace saw his chance. The fox was so bent on destroying Horace that he carelessly allowed another opening to develop. Horace lunged and once again disarmed his opponent. They both paused to watch the fox's blade spiral off into the night. "Surrender, Reynardo! It's all over now. You have no chance to win the day. Surrender peaceably and I will even plead for mercy from the Zorcerer on your behalf when I bring you to justice."

The fox snarled and drew a dirk from his boot, casting it at Horace in one smooth motion. It sliced through Horace's velvet doublet – and the shoulder beneath – but sailed out into the night. Horace glanced at his injury. "Only a flesh wound, fox. You're out of options. Surrender!"

Reynardo snarled, baring his vicious yellow teeth and threw himself at the pig.

Horace dodged at the last moment, throwing himself to one side. The fox was unable to stop himself in time and plunged over the roof. Horace watched him flail and pinwheel into the night, knowing there was nothing he could do to save the fox. If he had wanted to – no, a gentleman must be better than his foes. Horace turned away before he could see Reynardo be dashed against the rocks below. "Now, to put out that dratted light!" Horace muttered under his breath. He resheathed his swordcane and with a quick leap and thrust of his walking stick, Horace shattered the magical mirror. As the tinkling glass shards rained down on Horace's head, he felt an icy gust of wind blow out from it, and couldn't decide if he had actually heard a wolf's howl again echoing out into the night. With the mystic light extinguished, darkness fell across the rooftop, save for lightning dancing from cloud to cloud, though even that seemed to quickly diminish.

As Horace looked out to sea, he could begin to see gaps in the fogbank. The sea was still choppy, but as the fog began to thin, Horace noticed a large cargo ship - by the large silver lion's head on the ship's prow he knew it could only be the *Zolion's Grace* - in the rough surf below the cliffs. He lifted his magic monocle to one eye and, through it, could see magnified the tiny figures of the ship's captain and helmsman struggling to bring the ship about before it could be dashed against the rocks. Horace held his breath. He had already done all he could, but now that the ship's crew had succeeded in throwing off the mesmerizing magic of the mirror, they needed to steer the ship clear of the rocky cliffs. They continued to wrestle with the ship's wheel and rudder as Horace watched. The ship was caught in the surf and seemed doomed to crash against the rocks just offshore.

They were making no progress against the surf and the cause seemed hopeless. In a moment this last ship - and its precious cargo - would be broken against the rocks, the final victims of Reynardo and his fiendish plot. Horace's heart sank and a feeling of despair stole over him.

It occurred to Horace that perhaps there *was* one thing left that he could do. It was clear that the ship was being inexorably pulled toward shore. It would take a major wave - a veritable tidal wave - to push the ship back out to sea. But that wasn't going to happen. The current was dragging the ship *in*ward, not *out*ward. There *was* no wave that would travel from the shoreline outward, carrying the ship with it. Horace couldn't even summon such a wave; he was a master of enchantment, the transformation of one thing into another, not a master of wind and wave, surf and sea.

But a master enchanter – such as Horace Hogg, Esq. – *could* transform *himself* into such a thing. An enchanter like Horace, after all, contained a vast amount of magic potential. He himself could become that vast tidal wave and carry the *Zolion's Grace* back out to sea.

Yes. Such a thing was possible. Theoretically. Horace had never wrought such an enchantment before. This would, naturally, he knew, be his last spell – and his last act.

Horace marched to the edge of the cliff. He squared his shoulders and drew a deep breath. He began to summon his courage and the magic within him that might yet save the day, though, obviously, at great cost. As he prepared himself for his final, and perhaps his greatest act, Horace began to think about all the should-haves and might-have-beens, all the things he could have said or done, but had not. He thought about his lovely wife the Snow Witch, and the children they might have had together, but Horace realized that despite all the regrets he might have had, this was what he needed to do. To save a ship, and all aboard it, and all who would live because of its precious cargo? Ha! Horace laughed defiance into the wind.

Just then, he looked down at the ship just as the first rays of dawn glinted off the ship's leonine figurehead, looking almost like it had winked at him. Horace smiled to himself and prepared to . . . he paused again.

Wait, he thought. Wait just a minute. What in the–?

Dawn broke. The glimmer of light on the horizon became what Horace believed was the most beautiful dawn he had ever seen. Had he ever really *seen* a dawn – really *appreciated* it – in this way? No, he was forced to admit that he had not.

But it wasn't simply the beautiful light of dawn that drew Horace's attention. It was what accompanied the dawn: a calming of the sea. At first the waves just seemed a little less violent. Then the sea became flat.

Glassy.

Still.

Instead of a storm-tossed, raging sea, it now looked like a large lake or pond suitable for lazy paddling, or fishing, or just enjoying the day out on the water. Horace gaped, and watched the sun come up with one of the biggest grins of his life plastered across his snout.

It was turning out to be a beautiful day. Horace smiled and wiped away... well, a mote of dust must have gotten into his eye. He took in another long look at the water, and at the ship heading comfortably back out to sea to deliver a most precious cargo. Horace couldn't help but laugh as the joy of a second chance at life overcame him.

Having defeated Reynardo, the ship-breaker and servant of the Wolf Shaykosch, Horace Hogg breathed a deep sigh of relief, knowing that the *Zolion's Grace*, which carried the medicine to treat the victims of the Scarlet Plague, would make it to port safely. Even better, saving the ship, and the sick people of Rosso, had not required Horace's life. It was enough for him to know that he had been willing to do the right thing. He decided to set out for Rosso to figure out how the magical malady had broken out in the first place. . . but that's another tale.

THE END

Pussycat vs. Owl

by Chad Underkoffler

For Cathy

Once Upon A Time, in the Land of Zo...

There was the central kingdom of the Empire of Zo – styled as "Zo Proper" – ruled directly by the Zorcerer Himself (Herself? Itself?).

Zo Proper is a civilized, cosmopolitan land. The bottleblooms, greenfleece sheep, and fenjades that Zo Proper produced assured its wealth and power: all are useful, all are valuable, and all are needed in *every* home throughout the Land of Zo for a multitude of uses.

Zo Proper is where Jade City, capital of the Empire, lies. All of the kingdoms of Zo – Azul, Giallo, Rosso, Viola – contribute to the centrality of the capital. "All roads lead to Jade City" says the proverb, and this is true.

Jade City is also the home of the Zorcerer, and that fact cannot be taken too lightly. Neither can the fact that Jade City is the metropole of all scholars, sages, and indefatigable hunters of knowledge in all of Zo. It is to say that a single, simple bit of trivia can buy a fine dinner, with plenty of drink included. Be aware!

Within the emerald walls of Jade City lay two buildings of great import to this tale: the *Library of Lime University*, and the *Imperial Public Library* – two renowned institutions, filled to the brim with books, opinions, information, and Librarians to tend to the needs of their bookilicious denizens and knowledge-seeking patrons.

Let us take the latter into account first, because herein lies the heroine of our tale. The Talking Pussycat Ekateryna was the Prime Librarian of the Imperial Public Library. Her coloration was predominantly white, though the red-purple "eyepatch" around her left eye, the red-purple coloration of her ears, and the tabby-like red-purple hue of her tail hinted at a Rosson heritage (with, perhaps, some Violan ancestry?).

Smart, collected, straightforward, curious, Ekateryna loved books with a love that shook the heart – their dusty smell, their riffling pages, their weight within the paw. She pursued the goal of making the Imperial Public Library the *broadest* collection of volumes in the Empire. As Prime Librarian, she ruled her lesser Librarians with an iron fist, holding them to the greatest concern for both their charges (the books) and their patrons (the public). Still, she was fair, and nearly always had a grin of amusement upon her furry lips.

Her primary rival in bibliophilia was the Chief Librarian of Lime University, Marco by name, a Talking Owl, late of Azul. Marco was brilliant, excitable, subtle, and curious. He made the Lime University Library the *deepest* collection of volumes in the Empire, with an especial focus on tomes of magic. He managed his subordinate Librarians with a velvet glove, allowing them to research as they would; still, he was aware of all they did. An avian smile of amusement continually graced his beak. His coloration ranged from dappled dusky brown to purest white, and his gold-green eyes were penetrating and wise.

The rivals met – and argued! – often. Be it at an estate sale (where juicy books were up for the grabbing); at publishers' parties (where the latest literary works debuted); in dusty, deserted libraries (of long-dead bibliophiles like themselves); or in the numerous *cawfhauses* of Jade City (these establishments were dedicated to the brewing of the inedible Azulite *heatwheat* into the tasty beverage called *cawf*: the stimulating fluid favored by scholars and businessmen alike for its thought-speeding properties), the Pussycat and the Owl disputed one another.

Ekateryna and Marco debated with erudition and skill. Their insights were sharp, their knowledge vast, their arguments compelling. While sometimes one would have the advantage of the popular opinion of their audience over the other, this primacy fluctuated back and forth regularly.

A typical discussion would run in thus-wise fashion:

> EKATERINYA: The only gloss you have – in your entire Library! – on Rattleglaive's plays is that of Chouarete. This is a scholarly sin, Owl!
>
> MARCO: Ach, Cat: we do not have much call for the dramaturgical arts at the University.
>
> EKATERINYA: Not much call? Your scholars require a fully-rounded education!
>
> MARCO: Your tongue is as sharp as your claws, Prime Librarian. But know this: Lime University is dedicated to the mental enlargement of those who attend.
>
> EKATERINYA: How so? I fail to see, my dear birdbrain, how ignoring the discussions of the learned can possibly

aid your students.

MARCO: By giving our students the intellectual tools to make their *own* determination of the worth and meaning of Rattleglaive's amusements, completely on their own, we stimulate their analytical thought!

And so on.

Naturally, over time and following their chief advocates, a division developed between the patrons of the Imperial Public Library and the scholars of Lime University. Indeed (believe it or no!), it threatened to swamp the Jade City in riot. All of the scholars and the sages had united into factions supporting Ekateryna or Marco, fueling the fires of dissent. And this ridiculousness was over the proper way to prepare Northern Sea Turtle Soup. Jade City was a strange place in those days.

That riot is why they were both called to an audience with the Zorcerer.

The Smiling Soldier came to them, while they were hot in an argument over the deeper meanings of one of Maindroitelibre's proverbs ("well-done is better than well-said"). The Smiling Soldier was – and is! – the primary agent of the Zorcerer. Always affable, always in good humor, he strides and ranges at the Zorcerer's direction.

The Smiling Soldier arrived at the cawfhaus where the two librarians were arguing. His statement was simple: "You two are summoned to the Imperial Presence. Come now." His smile did not waver, but his tone was hard – much harder than his usual.

As loyal Zolanders, the pair could not refuse. They followed the Smiling Soldier out of the cawfhaus. They walked many avenues, passing fracases betwixt their respective supporters, before they reached the Citadel. There, they passed through the gates speedily. They entered the audience chamber of the Zorcerer without delay.

In the Reception Chamber of the Citadel, they stood before the Smaragdine Throne. A huge green fireball hovered above it – for that was the form the Zorcerer had chosen for this particular audience. The fireball crackled and flickered angrily, in sea-green hues.

THE PRIMACY OF ONE LIBRARY OR THE OTHER MUST BE ESTABLISHED, thundered the Zorcerer. ONE OF YOU MUST RISE ABOVE.

"But how, Lord?" asked Marco.

RECOVER THE LOST TOME.

"The Lost Tome, titled *Silver Beauty*, mighty Zorcerer?" asked Ekateryna. "None has had any knowledge of its whereabouts since the days of Emperor Zolion."

YES. COLLECT THIS STRAY VOLUME, AND PRIMACY WILL BE GRANTED.

And then the viridian fireball guttered out, leaving Marco and Ekateryna alone in the Reception Chamber and semi-darkness.

After a moment of silence, she said, "The Lost Tome?"

Marco said, "Indeed."

There was another moment of silence.

The Pussycat said to the Owl, "Ready?"

The Owl replied, "As ever."

"Let us hunt this book. Luck to you, but more luck to me."

"Harrumph!" exclaimed the Owl, but he nodded in agreement.

The two separated, each seeking to win the Quest set upon them.

Ekateryna pulled on the high, black, laced, *stompy* boots she favored: magical, of course. These Seven-league Boots allowed quick travel – a league is three miles, so each step of the Pussycat carried her twenty-one Zolander miles.

She first walked to her homeland of Rosso, to acquire an artifact of import.

Some days later, we find the Pussycat in Viola, hopelessly entangled within the branches of the *Willowthorn*. The Willowthorn is the oldest and tallest tree upon the face of Zo. Its weedy fronds entangle and pierce the unwary, wrapping up and holding them fast. The "happy sap" that coats the thorns induces euphoria (alongside the pain and restraint). Thus, the victims of the Willowthorn do not resist, and can only languorously and with great effort struggle against its embrace. Slowly, the Willowthorn consumes them as they chuckle and chortle.

Luckily, the Owl arrived soon after. His mighty wings carried him nearly as fast as the Pussycat's boots. He too had had to make a side-journey to acquire a useful tool, but had taken longer about his task than Ekateryna had. When he swooped down out of the twilight clouds to approach the Willowthorn, he saw the laughing Pussycat entangled in the tree's grasping branches. Always a gentleman, Marco quickly landed, drew his blade from his belt with one mighty talon, and freed his rival with three artful slashes. He caught her in his feathered wings as she began to tumble, giggling all the while, to the ground.

After a short time, Ekateryna recovered from the tree's happy sap. When Ekateryna's voice returned, she said to the Owl: "My thanks. I owe you a debt."

Marco again harrumphed, but a smile spread across his beak.

An odd though crossed the Pussycat's mind at that moment: the Owl looked very fine in his blue waistcoat and wide black leather belt (which bore numerous pouches and his now-scabbarded sword). She brushed the thought off, and said to him, "Also, I congratulate you on your astute choice of where to begin the hunt for the Lost Tome."

"As I, you as well," said he. "I suspect we must both be at the top of the Willowthorn to execute our endeavors."

The Pussycat nodded, a wry grin playing upon her lips.

The Owl quirked one of his tufted eyebrows. "May I offer you a lift?"

Atop the Willowthorn, the librarians stood side-by-side. The sun set in a glory of crimson, and purple night began to fall.

"As you were here first," said the Owl, "please make your assay."

From her satchel, Ekateryna removed a wooden cylinder with brass fittings.

"The Spyglass of the Wooden Pirate?" asked Marco. "I thought that it was in the Carmine Palace."

"No, featherhead, it's right here," laughed the Pussycat as she slapped the Spyglass into her palm. "The power of the Spyglass is to show hidden paths. Turn it thus–" a *click!* came from the object "–and it shows the **quickest** route; turn it thus–" a *clack!* came from the object "–and it shows the **safest** path."

"It worked well leading me here." She pulled the Spyglass open, and raised it to her eye. "Now, Spyglass, show me the course I must set to the place where the Lost Tome lies."

The Spyglass did nothing. The traceries of light that painted the lenses of it to show the path did not appear. She adjusted the device with a click, then lifted it to peer through again. Still nothing.

"Curious," said she. "There is no path."

Night had truly fallen by this point, but as the Pussycat and the Owl are both hunters in darkness, their cunning eyes were not much affected.

"Allow me to make my assay," said the Owl, drawing an object from his pocket with his foot. He showed it to her: a flat disk of glass, edged with some bluish material. Within its center, a silver needle floated.

Ekateryna blinked. "The Last Needle of the Blue Tailor?"

"Indeed. Also called 'the Compass of Heart's Desire.'"

"I thought the Stitchwitch, the villainous last of the hero's line, possessed that."

"She did; now I do. Despite her withered, bloodless heart not being able to form a pure enough desire to use this thing, she still charged me a Duke's ransom to acquire it."

"You bought it from her?"

Marco shrugged. "Villains tend to be greedy. Thus, good Zolander gold paved the way. Of course, she tried to take the gold and steal back the Compass..." He made a waving gesture with one wing. "But that is another tale."

"I look forward to hearing it some day, Chief Librarian," the Pussycat said with a smile.

The Owl returned her smile, then, holding the Compass flat in the palm of his talon, he addressed it. "Show me the bearing of my desire: the Lost Tome."

The needle within the glass began to spin wildly and silently.

"That's odd," muttered Marco. "Show me the bearing of my desire: my office at Lime University."

The needle made a ringing chime as it snapped to steadily point southeast.

Again, the Owl said, "Show me the bearing of my desire: the Lost Tome," and again, the needle spun aimlessly.

The stars began to grow bright in the velvet purple of the skies as the Librarians began to discuss these mysteries.

"Has the Lost Tome traveled outside the land of Zo?" asked the Pussycat.

"No, for our tools would show the path or bearing to it, even into an Otherworld," said the Owl.

"Well, to the closest gate to said speculative Otherworld."

"Harrumph. Granted."

"Are you sure?"

"Ha-harrumph! Indeed, Cat. Magical artifacts are my specialty, if you recall! This sort of thing is the benefit of a *deep* education."

Ekateryna snorted. "That reminds me. There's a typo on page 42 of your undergraduate thesis."

The Owl blinked at her. "*Seventeen Types of Azulian Wood Used in the Construction of Magical Artifacts of the Pre-Zorcerer Era?*"

"The Imperial Library recently acquired a copy."

Marco's eyes narrowed, and he stared at her.

She winked, then asked, "Perhaps the Lost Tome has been destroyed?"

"Perhaps, since the Spyglass shows no path. But the Compass is reacting, albeit strangely. If the Tome had been destroyed, neither should react."

The Moon began to rise in the far west of Zo.

"Can you be sure, Owl?"

"I assure you, Cat, this is--"

Suddenly, the needle of the compass chimed. The Librarians looked to it: it pointed due west.

"Ekateryna! The Spyglass!" cried Marco.

Quick as a flash, the Pussycat raised the Spyglass to her eye, and a line of red colored the lens, stretching from her feet to the rising Moon along the path of the quickest route. She twisted the barrel of the Spyglass with a clack! No blue line showed in the lens. Click! A red line, leading westward.

As the bottom edge of the Moon rose above the horizon, the line faded and the needle again spun wildly.

"It's on the Moon," said the Owl. "Of course!"

"Marco," Ekateryna said. "Professional Librarian courtesy insists I must warn you. The Spyglass says there is no safe path there, just a quick one."

"But isn't the life of a Librarian of Zo *always* full of such excitement, danger, hazard, risk, chance, and adventure?" he replied.

"Of course," she agreed. "And I wouldn't have it any other way."

The Sun of Zo rises in the east, and sets in the west. The Moon of Zo rises in the west, and sets in the east. Legend claims that they are lovers, who only meet once a month, beneath Zo, when the Moon is new. On rare occasion, they pass each other in the skies during the day. As their attentions turn away from Zo to focus on their celestial paramour, the world grows dark. As they embrace, an eclipse occurs, shining with the corona of their love.

After Marco flew them both to the moonlit ground, they parted ways at the base of the Willowthorn. He flew off, directly west, while she made a brief detour to the village of Breezedale to purchase necessary supplies for her long journey. The Owl would have a slight lead on the Pussycat in this Quest, but it could not be helped. Besides, her Boots would easily allow her to catch up with him – Marco could not fly as fast as the Boots could carry her.

After filling a backpack with rope, bread, wine, cheese, and other sundry supplies, she turned west and began to walk in her magic boots. She walked and walked. Miles upon miles, leagues upon leagues. Soon, she crossed the border of Viola and passed into the Kingdom of Giallo.

She walked and walked. Miles upon miles, leagues upon leagues. The grassy plains of Giallo unspooled beneath her feet. After a time, she crossed the border of Giallo – the very boundary of the Empire of Zo! – and entered the Pancake Plains.

She walked and walked. Miles upon miles, leagues upon leagues. The desert waste of the Pancake Plains rippled under the tread of her boots. Every seven leagues, she left a single footprint in the gritty sand. After a time, she came to a single spot of green, squatting in a circle of white-gray sand amidst the yellow-brown. An oasis.

A few palm trees, a flowering shrub or four, and some patchy grass rose from the curious white-gray sand. In the center, a pool of clear blue water. Next to the pool, a sleeping Owl. Marco.

"Fool," the Pussycat shook her head. "He obviously had no idea where he was perching."

She dropped her pack to the sand, and opened it up. Withdrawing a kerchief, she doused it with water from her waterskin before tying the cloth around her muzzle. Taking several deep breaths, she walked into the oasis, grasped the slumbering Owl with her paws, and began to drag him out of the circle of green.

Though Marco looked heavy, his hollow bones and fluffy feathers made him fairly lightweight. The Pussycat was able to pull him back to her waiting pack before the intoxicating fumes of the oasis' waters caused *her* to fall asleep, too.

She removed the kerchief from her face, and began to remove other items from her pack. Kindling, a small pot, a knife, a loaf of bread, a wedge of cheese, some dried fish, minced mice, a turnip, a carrot, celery, and other vegetables. She quickly built a fire, filled her pot from her waterskin, and began to make some stew while the Owl slept off the fumes.

He woke up just as the stew was bubbling nicely. "Wha–?"

"You really need to read more books about things that aren't magical artifacts, birdbrain. Do you know where you are?"

"Cat? How? I saw the oasis, and since I was tired and thirsty from all my flying, I landed and was going to take a drink of water."

"Be glad you didn't, Marco. If you'd actually *drunk* the waters of Oneiros' Oasis instead of just smelling them, you'd end up sleeping as long as Princess Morphea."

"The what in the who?" said the Owl, puzzled.

"Try to keep up." She pointed at the oasis. "Oneiros' Oasis. The waters give off a miasma that makes people fall asleep. This strange white sand is the crumbled, sandblasted bones of all its victims." She stirred the stew, which smelled wonderful.

"And Princess Morphea?"

"The Sleeping Princess of Rosso. Niece of King Glamorgan. Sleeping this past score of years, awaiting True Love's kiss." She ladled stew into a bowl for the Owl, and into another for herself. "It was in all the papers. Always is, when some Prince or Knight or whatever tries to get through the Briar Wall around Castle Slumber, and ends up hanging spiked on it. Do you even *read* the newspapers, birdbrain?"

Marco said nothing, and ate his stew.

Ekateryna laughed, and then fell to her own bowl.

After they had finished eating, the Owl said to the Pussycat, "You have repaid your debt to me by saving my life, not once, but twice over. First, you pulled me from the oasis; second, you preserved my life with this meal."

"Didn't you bring any supplies of your own?"

He shook his head sheepishly. "No, not much. I figured I could hunt on the way. I didn't expect the Pancake Plains to be so... barren."

The Pussycat scrubbed out her bowl in the sand, and indicated for the Owl to do the same. As he did, she said, "You see, Librarian, this sort of thing is the benefit of a *rounded* education."

He gritted his beak, but said nothing for a time.

When he did speak, he said, "Perhaps we should travel together?"

She agreed with a nod, but added, "I foresee a problem."

"Yes?"

"My Seven-league Boots carry me farther and faster than you can fly."

"This is true."

"Which brings to mind a question: how did you get to Oneiros' Oasis before I did? Your lead was not *that* large."

"Simplicity itself, my dear Pussycat. While I could fly directly over the Sea from the Willowthorn to Giallo, you were (alas!) landbound, and had to round the Bight of Wight."

"I see. I also stopped of in Breezedale for supplies," Ekateryna said. "A second question: how do you propose we travel together, given our variant rates of travel?"

Marco laughed. "Again, I have an answer. The other little toy I have brought with me, along with the Compass, is *this*." And, with a flourish, he withdrew an irregularly-shaped scrap of pea-green parchment from his pouch.

The Pussycat stared at the Owl, waiting for an explanation.

"This is the Folding Boat of Feem-to-la," explained Marco, as he began unfolding the small piece of paper into ever-larger pieces. His talons flickered as they spread the parchment out upon the sands, and the boat grew larger and larger.

"I would like to point out, pellets for brains, that this (if it has escaped your attention) is a *desert* – that is, *no water.*"

"Ha. Ha." The Owl finished a few final manipulations, and there before them on the sand sat a beautiful pea-green sailboat, easily large enough to hold both of them and their gear cozily. "Again, we come to the benefit of a *deep* education. The Folding Boat of Feem-to-la can travel on earth as well as water, faster than I can fly, but alas not as fast as your Boots can carry you."

He climbed into the stern of the boat, and held out a wing to help the Pussycat within. "Still wish to travel together?"

She put her paw on his wing, stepped inside, and then they were off, sailing towards the Edge of the Map.

As they sailed over the sandy wastes, the pair of Librarians bickered over academic and bibliographic topics, as usual. However, over time, their pointed words blunted and lost their edges. After only a few days, their debates became conversations. Ekateryna told him about the broader nature of the desert they scudded across, and various details she knew of its mysterious flora and fauna. For his part, Marco told her about the deeper history and powers of various famed artifacts, like the Spyglass and the Compass – and even a few secrets about her own Boots that she had never known!

Ekateryna found herself warming up to the Owl, despite his arrogance and his limited, cloistered knowledge of the wider world. He seemed to be growing a bit fonder of her as well.

Every night at moonrise, they would stand beside the Folding Boat and take sightings of the Lost Tome with Spyglass and Compass. Their path definitely led to the Moon.

One evening, however, probably only a day's journey from the Edge of the Map, the Owl began having problems with the Compass. With the Moon hanging hugely on the horizon before them, the needle within it waggled back and forth oddly. "I can't think what the problem is," said Marco. "Except–"

He closed his eyes, shook his head, and said softly. "Take a sighting for a safe path again, Cat."

"It hasn't worked yet, Owl," she protested.

"Still. Try one last time."

Clack! No safe path, limned in blue, appeared. "Nothing!" she said. She dropped the lens from her eye, turned to her companion, and saw something curious.

The Owl was looking at the Compass, then to the Moon, then to her, then repeating the cycle over again. As he noticed her looking at him, he sighed softly and placed the Compass back in his pouch. "The Compass cannot aid us further."

"Why?"

Marco said nothing for a moment. "I suspect we are too close... to the Moon." He shook his feathery head. "No matter. We will simply have to rely on the Spyglass."

The Pussycat quirked an eyebrow, but said nothing.

The next day, just after noon, found them at the Edge of the Map. Here, the land ended, and only an open expanse of sky stretched out before them. Tiny clouds speckled the dark blue sky below when they looked over the Edge.

"When the Moon appears, I should be able to step across using the Boots," said Ekateryna. "Stern's *Almanac* says that the gap between the Edge and the Moon is only a half-mile."

"An easy flight for me as well," said Marco.

So they waited. And waited. And waited.

Night fell. A glow from below presaged the approach of the Moon. The Pussycat felt butterflies in her stomach as she waited for it to rise.

The moment the rim of the Moon came into view, she started to take a step forward – but a strong wing closed around her arm, stopping her from stepping!

"What are you doing, Owl! Turning traitor?" she cried.

"No!" replied Marco, with some heat. "Look! Look at the gap!"

The empty space between the Edge and the Moon was larger than a half-mile. Larger than a league. Larger than seven leagues.

The distance from Zo to the Moon yawned at least thirty miles wide – ten leagues! If Ekateryna had stepped forward in her Boots, she would not have reached the Moon, but stumbled into the Blue to fall forever.

The Owl had saved her life.

The debated what to do for the rest of the night, even past moonset and into the dawn. The plan they finally decided upon was dangerous, but the only solution they could see: the Owl would carry the Pussycat over the Edge, leaping at nightfall but before moonrise, and they would glide – until the uprushing Moon caught them.

"I worry I am too heavy for you to carry, Owl."

Marco's eyes flashed as he said, "Do not worry, Cat. I will *never* drop you."

And thus, it came to pass. Night fell, the Owl grasped the Pussycat tightly in his strong talons, they leapt into emptiness, and glided down, down, down. The Moon spun up, up, up. In a shorter time than they expected, the pair of Librarians stood on powdery-gray moon dust, looking up at the multicolored rectangle of Zo.

Unfortunately, the Folding Boat would not work on the Moon – apparently it could only sail on the earth of Zo, not the earth of the Moon. (Marco grew excited, and started discussing the monograph he would write upon the subject until Ekateryna meowed at him to shut his beak.) The companions were forced to travel separately once again. Still, they met each night at Zo-rise (for so it seems, when one is on the Moon), and dined together under its strange, square light.

They, individually and together, fought their way through the strange, almost indescribably beautiful (yet bestial and violent) lunar beings – the Moth People, the Tiny Ape-Cats, and the Mantis-Goats were all equally irritating – that attempted to block their progress (but that is another tale). It took them nearly a week of walking and flight and desperate battle to reach Castle Terminus, which the Spyglass painted in red as the resting place of the Lost Tome.

Castle Terminus reared up on the very southern Edge (a viewer on Zo would call it the "bottom Edge") of the Moon. The "castle" was a fortress cleanly hewn out of Moon-mountain rock, into the gigantic shape of a laughing wolf's head. This obviously told the tale of who had stolen *Silver Beauty* lo those many years ago: *Shaykosch*.

Despite his scholarly excitement being aroused, Marco shuddered within his feathers. "The Gray Wind. The Wolf King. The Adversary. Death on Four Legs!" He whetted his beak with his tongue nervously. "Zolion's Courage, I hope he's dead or imprisoned elsewhere at the moment."

Ekateryna's fur was bristling at the sight of the Castle; slowly, she smoothed it down, and her tail went from bottlebrush back to its normal smooth fashion. "I believe he is. A pair of Heroes are said to have trapped him in a mirror or somesuch."

"How long ago?"

"Fifty years, give or take."

The Owl let out a sigh of relief. "Well, that gives us at least thirty years."

"How so?" asked the Pussycat. "I thought it usually took at least a century for the Wolf to escape and reform his last death or imprisonment."

"No, not usually. That's the *average* amount of time. Often, he's faster, sometimes he's slower. For example, with the imprisonment he suffered at the hands of the Witch Girl…" Marco expounded upon the history of Shaykosch's escapes and resurrections as they carefully walked up the narrow road to the gate, located within the stone wolf's jaws.

The gate was open. "It's a trap!" said the Pussycat.

"Indeed. No doubt the entirety of Castle Terminus is full of deadly and subtle traps." The Owl stroked the bottom of his beak with the flight feathers of his right wing. "Hm. Perhaps this would be the opportune time to use the Spyglass again?"

Ekateryna patted the Owl on the head. "Good thinking, birdbrain. The path here was all danger, and no doubt the paths within are all hazardous, but there must be a single one that is *least* dangerous." She removed the Spyglass from her pack and studied the wolf's head.

Clack! The safe path, shining blue, appeared, leading up to the left ear of the wolf's head. "Aha!" she cried. "Follow me." She stowed the Spyglass, and rapidly began to climb. Marco fluttered after her.

There was indeed a secret entrance within the wolf's ear. Cautiously, they entered.

The Wooden Pirate's Spyglass led them safely past innumerable dangers. These included pit traps; poisoned arrows; copper statues of the Gray Wind that spat thunderbolts; a gigantic rolling boulder; a narrow bridge over a bottomless canyon; walls of fire, stone, ice, thorns, and iron; and many more. Though the safest path was not without hazard, and the quick thinking or reflexes of each saved one or the other or both of them as they crept through the corridors. At one point, a waterfall thundered down and threatened to wash the Owl deep into the bowels of the Castle, but the Pussycat dove into the tumult and latched onto his waistcoat with her sharp claws, and was able to pull him free.

The pair of Librarians arrived intact (though somewhat soggy and bearing innumerable minor bumps and bruises and scratches and scorches) in a small round chamber, deep in the heart of Castle Terminus. They stood before a simple stone lectern, upon which sat a book, bound in pale white leather and chased with ornate silver fittings. Upon its cover, spelled out in silver runes, was the title: *Silver Beauty*.

Neither stepped forward immediately to take their prize. Instead, they started arguing about who should take it – but *not* in a fashion one would have expected at the outset of their Quest.

"Ekateryna, take it. Without your Spyglass, we would have never penetrated the defenses of Castle Terminus."

"No, Marco, *you* take it. Without you gliding us to the Moon, we would have never gotten here to use the Spyglass."

"No, Cat, *you* take it. Without you saving me at Oneiros' Oasis, we would have never…"

The tallying up of favors owed and debts repaid went on for some time. And on and on.

Eventually, the Pussycat browbeat the Owl into taking the Lost Tome. So he did, saying only, "Perhaps the Zorcerer will allow us to share in the primacy, for we shared in the getting of the prize."

Ekateryna smiled at having won the debate, of having gotten her way. However, she had the nagging suspicion she was forgetting something.

Using the Spyglass, they exited the Castle, avoiding further traps. They returned to the Edge of the Moon as quickly as they could. This was rather slow, but much safer than their approach, for the many beautiful lunar beasts that had attacked them on the way towards the Castle bowed down in peace as they saw the *Silver Beauty* in the flying Owl's talons.

Once at the Edge, they waited until after Zo-rise. The Owl once again glided them down to safety. Then, the Librarians used the Folding Boat to sail back across the wastes to the Empire. Though the Pussycat could have easily returned home much more quickly by using her Boots, she opted to remain and sail along with the Owl. Though saddened, and without much hope that the Zorcerer would accept Marco's offer of shared success for this Quest, she was not as upset as she would have been a month ago. Indeed, the experience had led her to cultivate greater respect for the Owl's knowledge, broadly limited as it seemed to be. And he seemed to have a much greater respect for her wider perspective of things. Perhaps that was enough: friendship between the head Librarians would lead to friendship between the Libraries and their patrons, and the arguments (and riots) would lose their sharp bite.

Soon enough, the pair of Librarians was again escorted into the Zorcerer's audience chamber by the Smiling Soldier. This time, hovering over the Smaragdine Throne was a huge lion's head, maned in purple clouds. It said nothing as the Owl stepped forward.

"The Quest is achieved, Zorcerer – here is the Lost Tome, *Silver Beauty*." (He slapped the pouch at his belt.)

THEN YOU HAVE WON THE PRIMACY, OWL.

"No, Lord," cried Marco. "The Lost Tome was only recovered by both of us working together. I ask that primacy between the Libraries be shared between them, in recognition of this."

The Zorcerer pondered a moment, and then said only one word.

NO.

The Owl's shoulders sagged as the Pussycat's heart fell, despite her expecting this result. Oh well, it wouldn't be so bad now, she thought. Now that we understand each other better.

Marco spoke again. "I was afraid of this response, Lord. Allow me a word with my companion." He turned to Ekateryna, and whispered. "I yet owe you a debt, for saving my life at the Oasis.

Here!" And a talon dipped into his pouch, pulled out the Lost Tome, and thrust it into her paws. He stepped aside and put his wings behind his back.

Shocked, she could say nothing as the Owl addressed the Zorcerer again. "Lord, the right of primacy rightly belongs to the Prime Librarian of the Imperial Library."

The misty purple lion's head nodded, saying – SO IT SHALL BE – and faded away.

Ekateryna finally recovered her voice. "Why, Owl? You are equally worthy of the position. Why use the flimsy excuse of your debt to me (which I am sure has been repaid many times over in the course of our adventures anyway) to award me rule over your Library?"

"Three reasons, Cat. One: you are a skilled scholar of wide knowledge, which is very valuable in this world, possibly more important than my focus on depth (though I am sure we will argue this in the future). Two: You would have eventually found a way onto the Moon yourself, so my contribution there should not be overvalued and the usefulness of your Spyglass was paramount. And third…"

He pulled the Compass from his pouch, and laid it flat upon his foot. "Show me the bearing of my desire."

The Needle within rang as it snapped to point directly at Ekateryna.

"Third: I *love* you," he said.

The Owl's words shook the Pussycat to her very heart as she suddenly realized that she *loved* him as well. Tears (of joy) welled up in her eyes at this new understanding. Henceforth, their relationship would be one of love – fraught with squabbles and disagreements and cross-purposes, of course – yet all underlined with amity and care and respect.

She reached out. Paw on wing, they walked from the audience chamber into the bottlebloom-scented Zo night, already discussing – with contention and laughter – the changes she would wreak upon the relationship between the Libraries.

Ekateryna and Marco took many more journeys together in search of books and knowledge, as well as for simple enjoyment. Their famous boating jaunt down the Verdan River to the Sea in their pea-green boat (equipped with honey, money, a guitar, and a Runcible Spoon), and what happened afterward . . . well, that's another tale.

THE END

The Bespectacled ~~Boy~~ *Man* Returns to Zo

by Chad Underkoffler

Once Upon a Time, in the Land of Zo…

I stepped through my grandma's elf-door and exited out of a crappy tavern in east Giallo – the Stone Plow. A nothing place, sitting in a crossroads across from a broken-down smithy.

Relatively close to the border with Zo Proper, it was still essentially a dive bar. I had no interest in sampling their ale or wine. I'd been here before, years ago. Zo was a bit more lax on serving children alcohol than the Waking Worlds, but they still kept a close eye on them to see if they got silly. (I'd gotten silly, back then, and there was a witch and a Talking Ear of Corn to deal with. No joke. Embarrassing.)

One should never allow an eight year old with a penchant for violence get drunk.

I was glad to see they finally had repaired the chimney, though.

No matter: I was back in **ZO**!

I sniffed the clean air. Perfect weather, as always. Even when there were storms, they were *perfect* storms, if you know what I mean. No gray leaden days. Never. (Well, unless they were *perfectly* gray leaden days. Whatever.)

I looked at the Talking Animals walking around the crossroads. People – Talking Animal people and a few Humans – would come here in trade or on journeys. I sat down on a hitching post in front of the Stone Plow and just people-watched for a time.

There was the Frog in his fine waistcoat and silver watch chain, strutting around like a popinjay; either the local mayor or some visiting semi-noble idiot. A dour Turkey wearing only a blue leather vest – an Azulite trader, I'd bet – fussing with his wagon full of goods. Some half-dozen faeries, swarming around the inn's stable, and who knows what for.

I took a deep breath.

I felt the subtle thrum of magic running through every aspect of the world. Glorious. Amazing. I took another deep breath and stepped into the inn's yard.

And, in the sunlight, I discovered a problem. I was still dressed in the fashion of my earlier visits: crazy schoolboy flavor – short pants, vest, beret. All upscaled to fit my adult body. Woof! I looked more or less ridiculous. (Well, moreso than usual.)

There was a weight in my left shirt pocket. I took it out, and it was the SuperSpectacles that Clockwright Secundus had made me long ago, and bound to my soul. It was good they were here. I took off my Otherworld glasses and replaced them with the SuperSpecs.

Even without the SuperSpecs, I knew that my clothing would be a problem. So I spoke the "Appropriate Attire" spell I learned in Magic 201 at Lime University.

The scent of ozone and copper, normally the aroma of magic, was strangely invaded by a hint of mint.

I looked around, and yes, there was a hint of green amidst the purple and the brown lights that played around me. Green.

Green.

I had just done *zorcery*.

What in Zolion's Name?

Long bottle-green coat. Pale green pantaloons. (Dang it; I prefer trousers.) White poet's shirt and similar colored stockings. Vest of hunter green, with black trim. Black boots. Dark green fedora (fedora?) on my head. Saber at my side. Weight in both my left chest pocket and right pants pocket.

- *Left chest*: A wallet with a badge and an ID for the Imperial Secret Service.
- *Right pants*: A pouch full of gold, maybe a hundred florins.

I had expected to change into the clothes of a normal yeoman, and now I was a fancy gentleman. Who was also armed. Who was also a spy.

What have I gotten myself into?

And, like magic, across the street an old friend suddenly appeared.

*   *   *

Ilsa Hund, the most accomplished minstrel of the Five Realms of Zo, set down her staff and pack and sat down with me as I re-sat on the hitching post.

"Jonathan," she began. "You got... tall. And even more

185

handsome." The Talking Dog smiled at me.

I felt my cheeks flush. "As you say, dear lady."

"What brings you to Giallo?" she asked.

"Called to adventure, I suppose." I sniffed deep of the air of Zo. "It's good to be back."

"It's good to have you back, Jonathan." There was a look, a twinkle, in her eyes.

My SuperSpecs whirred, and I saw she was holding a secret. Okay, not really a secret, but something secret-ish. "What?" I asked, flatly.

Ilsa huffed. "I like it better when you're all more polite and mannered." She was faking indignation, though – that was obvious.

I crossed my arms and stared at her.

She sighed, and said, "Okay, okay. You're obviously the one this omen is for."

"Omen?"

"A verse no one can match to a song, but sounds like it should."

I nodded.

She continued, singing. "The Robin knows the Secret Song. / The notes have sounded for years along." She stopped. "That's all we have."

"That's odd."

"And cryptic."

I smiled. "Yup, sounds like an adventure."

She smiled back.

"Especially since the Zorcerer seems to be taking a hand in my visit."

Her eyes widened. "What?"

I showed her the secret badge, and told her of the influence of zorcery on my simple spell.

She shook her head. "Jonathan, this adventure might go deeper than expected."

I nodded. "Of course. I'm older now, and adventures aren't so simple. It makes sense."

Ilsa looked at me in a very strange way, then simply said, "Give us a squinch."

I hugged her, she hugged back.

She whispered into my ear, "Be careful, Bespectacled B – Bespectacled Man. I'd hate to see you come to harm."

*   *   *

I thought a bunch about having accessed zorcery, however inadvertent.

Zorcery is weird and of its own. I've been around it enough to note its (in the moment) chaotic effects, but also its (in the long-term) structured and sustainable effects. There are whole graduate classes at Lime University dedicated to analyzing it. And yet, after centuries, no definitive answers.

I thought I had a whisp of an idea, but it always vanished when my mind tried to grasp it. Oh, well.

Accepting the mystery of the Zorcerer's interest as a thing, I finally stepped onto the road to truly begin my adventure.

(Yes, that sounds very glorious, yes? But it was twenty miles of heat and dust before anything interesting happened. Be warned. Remember to take extra water.)

*   *   *

I was passing some type of new cactus on the road – it wasn't Saguaro, it wasn't a cactus that existed in the Waking Worlds, or in my earlier travels through Zo. I called it Dart Cactus (which was a neat move, differentiated it versus Vampire Cactus, found in the south of Giallo).

Long story short: I got shot by idiot foliage, and it hurt. It's a blot on my resume. Who knew smearing honey on your skin would stop them from shooting you? Didn't expect it; paid the price.

Dart Cactus shoots you a bajillion times. Vampire Cactus sucks your blood and rejuvenates itself. (That is, your health is stolen for their health.) Stupid Zo plants.

*   *   *

I held my blade at the Coyote's throat. He was the alpha. Three of his pack lay dead around me.

"Why?" I asked.

"The Wolf told us to kill everyone coming south on this road." The Coyote growled, but I pressed my blade until he started to bleed.

My SuperSpecs whirred and locked onto truth.

"Will you go, or are you bound to his orders?"

"We will go. We are unbound." The Specs agreed.

188

"Good. Trifle with me again, and I will have your guts for garters."

The Coyote laughed. "Who talks like that? 'Guts for garters'?"

"I do. Now, scatter."

The remaining pack of coyotes disappeared.

"This is not a usual fairy tale," I said to myself. "Something's wrong."

*   *   *

A whisp of a song; partially unheard lyrics, all caught in the net of a dream.

Ilsa had been **right**.

*   *   *

The cygnet girl – the young Swan child – was terribly sick. The slash on her wing was angry and red, and she was running a bad fever. SuperSpecs confirmed it: infection. Her mother hovered around: worried, fluttering.

Under my breath, I cursed. "By Zolion's sacred mane, why didn't I pay more attention to sickness rather than injury in Healing 101?" I could easily use magic to heal a battle-wound or an accidental injury, but I had little grounding or experience at healing sickness.

"Sir?"

I shook my head. "Never mind." It was time to rely on Otherworld Red Cross and Boy Scout knowledge, rather than

189

magic.

I looked at the cygnet's mother. "I need a kettle of boiled fresh water, some cloth compresses dipped in cool water, and some willow bark, about a handful. And a mortar and pestle. Garlic would be good, to, a bulb or two. Also some strong spirits – whiskey, if you have it."

The Lady Swan nodded and began to collect what I'd asked for.

*   *   *

In an inn somewhere in Rosso, I saw the Wolf in my mirror.

He paused, to laugh at me.

My SuperSpecs whirred and I stared at Him.

Then He was gone… but I had His signature locked.

*   *   *

The Robin is in Bugburg. It came in a dream.

*   *   *

"Stand and deliver!" shouted the goblin, at the head of about a dozen of his fellows.

My SuperSpecs whirred, and I saw they were Dawn Goblins. You can tell by the shape of their ears.

I stopped walking down the road. "Well, I'm standing. What is it I'm supposed to deliver?"

He had an axe, and flourished it as he said, "Your purse, your wallet, your coin – or we will kill you!" The other goblins laughed and cheered.

My head tilted to the right about 45 degrees, and I stared at the lead goblin. "Really?"

The stare threw him a little bit. "Really, yes!"

"Hm."

He became infuriated with my delay. "This is not a complex choice! Throw down your wallet and we let you live! What else could you be thinking of?"

In cold, clipped tones, I replied. "I'm thinking the last time some goblin bandits held me up, there were only four of them. And I was fifteen years younger, armed only with a brace of daggers. And I didn't know any magic. And I still painted the Southern Highway with their life's blood."

I drew my saber, and said a word infused with magic. "*Voltari.*" Purple and green lightning (green again? the Zorcerer and I would be having a chat, soonish!) crackled around my blade.

I returned my head to the vertical, and said only one word to the goblin band. "Run."

*   *   *

"...and they ran, but I neglected to properly balance the Catch of my magic, so my saber is now a lump of slag."

The Talking Badger smith grunted. "That'll happen." He poked at it with one claw. "Give you a copper for the slagged steel."

"Done," I said. "But the fenjade in the pommel is worth at least two silvers."

He nodded. "As you say, sir."

I snorted. "Don't 'sir' me, Brannigan. You knew me as a stripling youth."

The Badger smith smiled. "'Stripling youth'? Who talks like that?"

"I do, you mangy old cuss." I looked around the smithy. "Would you have a spare sword anywhere's about?"

"I might, I might. But you're not gonna like it."

I frowned. "Why?"

"Shortsword."

I groaned. "I hate shortswords."

"Ayup."

I fumed a bit. "What's the quality?"

"Vang's work. Got it in trade for a spring-yoke."

I fumed a bit more. "Let me see it."

"Ayup." And Brannigan moseyed over to a pile of iron and uncovered a shortsword in a tooled leather sheath. Then he handed it to me.

I drew and looked down the blade. It was true. And, SuperSpecs assured me it was sharp as all get-out. I resheathed the blade.

"I don't like it, but I need it."

"Ayup." The badger pulled out a long, thin clay pipe, and tamped it with tobacco.

"Fair trade for the slag and the fenjade?" I asked.

The badger lighted his pipe. "Ayup. Though I might be making out a bit more than usual on the deal."

I laughed. "Fair enough. How about a meal and a space to sleep in for the night? Will that square us enough for your conscience?"

"Fair enough, good sir." The badger smiled.

* * *

She was a Talking Goat, her name was Lydia, and she had five kids. They would starve within the week.

I gave her forty golden florins, about half of what I had left. It was all I could do. It would have to be enough.

I walked on.

* * *

I entered the Bugburg police station. Talking Dog desk sergeant. Great.

"I need to talk to the prisoner," said I.

The Dog huffed and puffed for awhile, and I pulled out the wallet with my Imperial Secret Service badge.

That stopped the huffing and puffing.

I was shown into a room that held a Talking Robin.

"You know a secret that the world needs to know."

The Robin nodded.

"I believe I am the one your song needs to be sung at."

The bird looked doubtful. "Not... the... world." it said, through gritted beak. "Just... you."

I pondered for a second, then spoke. "Okay. Just for me. Sing, please."

The bird sang the Secret Song, and I released him.

*   *   *

Building the stone wall for the Talking Horse herder was hard, but honest work.

"I bet we moved and mortared a hundredweight of rocks."

The Horse – Esteban – agreed. "Many thanks, traveler."

I looked out on the herd of sheep. "Esteban, does it bother you as a Talking Animal, dealing with Dumb Animals? Responsible for their life, care, and death?"

The Horse scratched his chin with a hoof, then snorted and fluffled out his mane. "A little." He pawed the ground. "But one must work and live." His tremendous head shook. "None of us choose to be born Talking or Dumb Animals. We just work with what we're given." He snorted again. "I try to treat my Dumb cousins as I'd want to be treated. That's the best I can do."

I nodded. "I see that. Thank you."

"There are cakes, ale, and a bucket of wash-water for you," said Esteban.

"My sincere thanks," I said, and bowed.

*   *   *

"You are all idiots," I told the mob.

They screamed and cheered their stupid slogans. They were riled up.

I did the "Cylinder of Protection" spell I learned in Magic 201. Jeez, I need to buy Professor Marcus (a fine old Ferret) an ale at some point. That class has ended up being *remarkably* useful. The green energy of zorcery crackled alongside the usual blue.

I turned to the visitors from Othersea, who happened to be eight foot tall Talking Centipedes (and at least one Talking Ant, but she was tricksy – never quite got a good glimpse of her). "Talking Insects are rare in the Five Realms. Please excuse the most stupid of our citizens."

The lead Centipede was of a reddish tone. Her mandibles clicked at me. "Thank you, Imperial Diplomat of th—"

That's when I stopped her. "No, milady. I am not here on official business, of any sort. I am simply a gentleman of... (heck, why not?) Otherworld, and I saw you being wronged."

Her faceted eyes rotated at that. She said nothing.

"I have sent for an Imperial courier; you will have your diplomat soon enough."

Inscrutable.

"Well, milady, I must deal with the mob. Good wishes to you in your efforts, provided they do not harm Zo."

She nodded. "Much wellness to you, in the same regard." She paused and clacked her mandibles again. "You are a strange mammal."

I laughed. "Indeed, milady. I am even considered strange among my mammal-kin." I bowed, and walked out to deal with the mob.

. . .

It took 27 minutes, and I didn't murder anybody. WIN!

$$* \quad * \quad *$$

The Robin knows the Secret Song. / The notes have sounded for years along.

$$* \quad * \quad *$$

I think I'm finally getting a handle on zorcery.

It's not so much !Ω蝙蝠Δ, as ¿우주선φ

$$* \quad * \quad *$$

"That rock is wrong," I said to the mason.

The Human mason rubbed his jaw, and grunted agreement.

My SuperSpecs whirred and focused on the flaws in the block of marble. I pointed out each problem to the craftsman, then said, "Frankly, Dawid, you're better off getting a fresh piece rather than trying to fix this one."

Dawid sighed. "It's an expense I can ill afford."

Then I sighed. "I could try to use some magic to fix the flaws. I don't much like doing that, but if you're in a pickle, I'll do it."

Dawid smiled. "'If you're in a pickle'? Who talks like that?"

"I do. Now, stand back."

*   *   *

In a thunderstorm, huddling under a rowan tree, I finally understood: *Zorcery is the power to change the rules.*

*   *   *

Walking up the dusty road, I finally entered Zo Proper, through the Emerald Gate, from the south.

I made for the coffee-shop I liked, just outside the borders of Lime University.

And who do you think was there, outside, on the wrought iron chairs and tables?

I set my pack down. "Marquis, Grandmaster, and Your Majesty." I smiled. "Or, more familiarly, Tommy, Horace, and Q. Good to see you again."

"Please sit, Jonny," said the Marquis of Carabas.

Horace Hogg stood, bowed, and snapped for a waitron. He had a questioning look, but said nothing to me, as a gentleman should. "Rosson coffee, strong, please. And a pitcher of cream, and a loaf of the brown sugar." The waitron's eye widened at this extravagance, but said nothing.

Quellabaum, King of the Winged Monkeys, just rustled his feathers.

A coffee appeared for me, in a glazed mug, along with a chair. I indulged myself in both before speaking.

"Gents, it's good to see you."

Lots of aye-ayes and well-mets came from the table.

"Horace, I hear you fought the Wolf, became ennobled, married the Snow Witch, and have a child on the way. Congratulations!"

The pig smiled, and said nothing. Curious. For later.

"Our pig is somewhat shy," said the Marquis of Carabas. "Doesn't like to bugle out his deeds."

Quellabaum snorted. "Idiot."

"Apparently, I am back for an adventure." I offered.

"Finally," said Quellabaum. He pulled out a cigar and lit it with a fire cantrip.

"Finally *what*?" I asked.

He puffed and slid his bowler (the crown of the Winged Monkeys, if you believe it, encircled by a golden band) back upon his head. "Bespectacled Man, what is your true name?"

"Jonathan Alexander King," I replied.

He puffed his stinky cigar, then said, "And that would make your initials what?"

I frowned, bored by this idiocy. "J-A-K."

"And that spells, or sounds like…?"

I pondered for a second, but Horace was faster. "JAK equals 'Jack'!"

Oh, dear Zolion. No. No!

The King of the Winged Monkeys leaned in, and blew a cloud of blue-grey smoke into my face. "How many adventures have you had, and I know you triumphed in all of them."

I whispered, "Seven."

"How many other heroes of Zo had that many?" he snapped.

"Well, the Wooden Knight and the Witch Girl each had three, and the Owl and the Pussycat had two each, and the Gingerbread Knight—"

A clawed hand, grabbed my shirt at the neck, and pulled me up to stare at violet eyes.

"Stop. Lying. To. Yourself."

Then he dropped me, like a bag of flour.

That is exactly when it hit me – I knew why I was back in Zo, and why I had had the adventures along the way.

"Friends, we need to see the Zorcerer."

*   *   *

"Smiling Soldier."

"Bespectacled Man."

"Please open the gate; I believe we have a scheduled audience with the Zorcerer."

The Smiling Soldier said nothing, but opened the gates.

I walked in, trailed by the Cat, the Pig, and the Winged Monkey.

In the Great Hall, I cried, "ZORCERER!"

And that giant flame-ball of green fire showed up.

"**WHO DARES?!**" said the flaming ball.

"Bespectacled Man," I said. "And friends."

"**OOH, IT'S TIME,**" burbled the ball.

"Make yourself presentable, ok?" I grinned. My companions were shocked with the off-handed way I addressed the Zorcerer.

"**DONE,**" and the ball of fire guttered out.

A tug on my sleeve. "Jonny, what are you doing?" asked the Marquis of Carabas.

Quellabaum said, "He's doing what he was brought back into Zo to do."

Horace just nodded.

An old lady, silver-white hair in a bun, walked out on the stage. "Josephine Amanda Carpenter." She held out her hand.

I took it and laughed. "J-A-C. Another Jack."

The old lady smiled.

"Jonathan Alexander King, milady." I also kissed her hand. I'm old-school; deal with it.

"Are you ready and willing to be the Zorcerer?" Josephine asked.

"Willing, yes; ready – how could I be?"

She laughed.

Then took a deep breath. Green lightning gathered around her.

Then said, "It's gonna hurt a little bit."

"Of fricking course." I smiled.

She smiled again, and said, "I pass the mantle of the Zorcerer to Jonathan Alexander King. *Now*."

*   *   *

It *really* fricking hurt.

Ow.

Owowowowowo!

*　　*　　*

Becoming the Zorcerer was becoming everything.

I cannot describe it.

Insane amounts of power; insane amounts of exposed nerves.

It's an. . . okay job, but I wouldn't recommend it.

*　　*　　*

And now I was a green fiery head-ball.

"JOSEPHINE?"

"Here."

"TOMMY?"

"Here, Zorcerer."

"HORACE?"

"This is weird, Jonny, but I'm here."

"Q?"

"I knew this was coming from the first day you set foot in Viola."

"YES, YES, YOU'RE VERY WISE. JERK."

I modulated my voice down to human levels. "Okay. Josephine is gonna go back to her time... 1922?"

"1923, Zorcerer."

"Cool. Be careful about futzing with the timestream."

"What's futzing?"

"Altering. Messing with. Interfering."

She nodded. "Not more than is necessary to protect my family and friends."

I pondered, and sent my zorcery senses along the path she was intending. After a quick second, I nodded. "Fair enough."

Then I turned to other matters.

"Horace, we need to talk about the Wolf."

"Agreed, Majesty."

"Cut that 'Majesty' stuff out in about a week or so."

"Absolutely, *Majesty*."

I smiled. "Jerk." I gathered my thoughts, now more wide-ranging and numerous than ever before. "I want an analysis of the actions of the Wolf in the mirror. Three days."

"It will be done, Zorcerer." And the gentleman pig enchanter withdrew.

There was something like an itch on my back. "Q, something's weird in the northwest border of Viola. Not Otherworlder… feels like trolls."

"On it," and he flapped away.

I felt like I wanted to sneeze… from my elbow.

"Thomas?"

"Yes, my liege?"

"Keep on keeping on, and familiarize me with the current scuttlebutt. Pay attention to Rosso right now. Something is brewing there."

"By your command, Zorcerer." The cat left.

I turned back to Josephine. "Anything else I should know?"

She shrugged. "Nope, you've got it pretty well handled. You have experience here, and friends, and a good heart. You'll be a fine Zorcerer." She kissed me on my fiery cheek. I didn't burn her. How could I?

"Thank you."

Pause.

"Josephine, I'll open the portal for you."

She shook her head. "No, all I have to do is find that tree in Azul..."

"THE ZORCERER WANTS TO TEST HIS POWERS!" I rumbled.

The old lady laughed. "You're *just* as annoying as I was. Go ahead."

I pulled together purple and green, and wove them into a needle, then I pierced reality, and sent Josephine back to her own time.

*   *   *

Being the Zorcerer is weird. But, it's a good kind of weird.

Welcome to Zo.

(NEVER) THE END

www.ingramcontent.com/pod-product-compliance
Lightning Source LLC
Chambersburg PA
CBHW030312200626
46816CB00002BA/871